SHADOW OVER
THE
BACK COURT

SHADOW OVER
THE
BACK COURT

MATT CHRISTOPHER

BellaRosaBooks

SHADOW OVER THE BACK COURT
ISBN 978-1-933523-37-8
2008 Reprint Edition by Bella Rosa Books

Previously Published in the U.S.A. by Franklin Watts, Inc.
First hardback edition: 1959.

Printed in the United States of America on acid-free paper.

BellaRosaBooks and logo are trademarks of Bella Rosa Books

10   9   8   7   6   5   4   3   2   1

CHAPTER 1

THE BALL slapped the floor inches from Jeff's foot and bounced up into Eddie Russell's waiting hands. Jeff spun, the sweat shining on his bare shoulders. He jabbed hard at the ball. But Eddie, guard on the jay-vees' team, feinted an overhand pass, then bounced the ball under Jeff's right arm.

Jeff whirled in time to see Gil Baker catch the ball, pivot, and shoot for the basket. The ball banked against the backboard and fluttered through the hoop. It was Gil's favorite shot, and he seldom missed.

"Thatago, Gil, boy!"

Jeff shook his head. He'd never make first team that way.

A second-string player tossed in the ball from behind the out-of-bounds line. The first team rushed down court to cover their basket. The second team dribbled the ball down cautiously. Beyond the center line Dick Mizner, who had the ball, stopped and passed to Jeff.

Jeff dribbled down the side line, then stopped quickly and shot a quick overhand pass to Sam Bullick, who stood free under the basket. Sam caught the ball, turned, and tried for a lay-up.

Somebody rushed in and hit his hand. The ball banked into the net but the whistle shrilled. Coach Stu Cochran called a foul on the play and gave Sam the ball.

"Watch that charging, Ike," he warned a slender redhead.

Sam missed the shot. Jeff stretched high for the rebound and caught the ball on his finger tips. He jumped, arching the ball just over the rim of the basket. The ball riffled through the net.

Sam tapped him gently on the hip. "Nice shot, Jeff."

Jeff's heart sang as he bolted down the court toward the other basket. But a bucket now and then was not enough to assure him of being a regular player on the first team. Eric Wilson and Bill Godell were good, too. Those were the two he had to beat out—especially Eric.

Jeff passed the center line and turned. Gil Baker brought the ball down the court. He passed to Eric. Eric dribbled in fast, going through three players. Suddenly he pulled up straight, lifted the ball high over his head, snapped his wrists. The ball struck the backboard and banked through the hoop.

Jeff looked at Eric. Not a hair on that shiny black head seemed to have moved out of place. Eric caught Jeff's eye. He winked, and cracked a thin triumphant smile. Jeff looked away, resentment flaring in him. If anybody could get under Jeff's skin it was Eric.

The second team tossed in the ball from out of bounds. Jeff took it, dribbled across the center line, then passed to Sam. Quick as lightning Eric leaped forward, struck the ball from Sam's hand, and dribbled all the way down the court to his basket. Jeff raced after him.

Eric leaped for the lay-up. The ball struck the backboard, rolled halfway around the rim, and dropped over the outside edge. Jeff and Eric jumped for the rebound. Jeff felt Eric's shoulder brush hard against him. Jeff caught the ball, pulled it down, and started to dribble away. Eric sprang like a cat in front of him and clawed at the ball. Jeff stopped. He saw a teammate run up behind Eric. Jeff faked a throw, bringing the ball over his head with both hands. Eric leaped. Jeff came down on his heels, whirled on his pivot foot, and swished a pass to Sam who was streaking for the basket. Sam caught the ball, bounded high for a lay-up, and made it.

Jeff turned and ran down court, a faint pleased smile on his lips. He had fooled Eric completely on that play.

The whistle blew.

"That'll be it for this morning," said Coach Cochran. "Take your showers."

Jeff took a deep breath. He wiped the sweat off his brow with his finger tips and headed for the basement. On the way down the concrete steps he yanked off his Number 8 jersey. He was tired. Lee Mattoon, the tall center for the first team, trotted up beside him.

"You did all right, Jeff," Lee said. "I think you'll make it."

Jeff smiled.

"Think so, Lee?"

Lee shrugged.

"You looked pretty hot out there today."

"Thanks," said Jeff.

He was trying hard for a position on the first team. Last year as a freshman in high school he had warmed the bench most of the time. He was going to work harder this year. Nothing was worse than sitting on the bench throughout a game, hopefully waiting for the coach to put you in—and then, when he did, to play for only half a minute.

He had to make first team this year. It wasn't only because he wanted to play basketball more than anything else, but there was another reason, too. Jeff's brows pulled together, leaving tiny worried lines just above his nose, as he thought of something his father had said recently:

Basketball is a waste of time!

Jeff's father, a supervisor at the Dunnigan Electronics Laboratories, had said other things, too: You're going to school to learn, Jeff. You're a Dooley. Dooleys are creators, builders. They're men who have helped to shape the world. They've never had time to spend on foolish things like baseball, football, or basketball.

Mr. Dooley wasn't mad when he said those words. He had said them as he would say anything else. But he had meant them, and that's what hurt.

That had been two weeks ago, when basketball season started. But something that was so close to your heart couldn't be broken with so easily. Basketball was like that for Jeff. He couldn't keep away from it. Ever since the first word got around that players were needed for the junior varsity, he was in the thick of it. He belonged like a frog belonged to a pool.

Jeff reached the locker room. He pulled open his locker door and hauled out a towel. Bruce Parker, a first stringer for the jayvees, began to sing in his deep husky voice. Bruce couldn't carry a tune, but he loved popular music and knew the words of most of the songs. Right now his off-key singing brought a grin to Jeff's lips and made him forget, for a while, those strong words of his father's.

The needle spray of the shower felt good. Jeff dried himself, dressed, and was combing his hair when he heard Lee Mattoon say:

"No! You can't do that to us, Gil!"

Jeff turned. Others who had heard turned, too.

"Do what, Lee?" said the coach, who was standing in the doorway. "What's the matter?"

"Gil's quitting the team," said Lee.

Jeff started.

"Quitting the team?" Coach Cochran bolted from the doorway. He walked between the benches filled with players and sweat-soiled uniforms, and stopped in front of Gil. Gil, who was an inch shorter than he, was buttoning up his shirt.

"What's this, Gil? Is it true?"

"I'm thinking about it, coach," said Gil softly. "I haven't definitely made up my mind yet."

"What's your reason? Why do you want to quit?"
Gil reached for his jacket.

"I'm falling down in my studies."

"What subjects? Any one in particular?"
Gil shrugged.

"All of them. I flunked a test yesterday."

The coach looked directly at him, then turned to the other players in the room.

"I'm sorry to hear that. I was figuring—" He paused, looked back at Gil. "Never mind. I'll talk to you about this later."

Silence filled the room as the coach turned on his heels and walked out. Jeff could hear his feet slowly plod up the stairs and then fade.

"Study nights, Gil," Bruce Parker suggested. "Can't you study nights?"

"I do, a little. But I'm poohed out by the time I can sit down and study. I can't think straight. I'm not like Jeff, or some of you other guys. I have to read a page three or four times to remember what I've read. You guys don't."

"So what does that prove?" said Eric. "You want to be a college professor or something?"

"I want to be an engineer," Gil answered in his quiet voice.

"A train engineer?" Eric laughed. "You don't have to go to college for that."

Somebody laughed. But the remark wasn't funny. Jeff didn't find it funny, nor did Lee Mattoon.

"There's mechanical engineering, and there's civil engineering, and other kinds too," said Lee. "Don't wisecrack. Gil knows better what he wants than any-body else."

"Oh, I was only kidding," said Eric. "I didn't mean anything, Gil."

"That's okay, Eric," said Gil. He pulled on his calf-skin gloves and headed for the door. Lee and Bruce followed him out. "See you guys tomorrow."

"Yeah. See you." The words fell softly from Jeff's lips. He gave the dial on the locker door a twist and walked out behind Sam.

So Gil was quitting the team because he couldn't keep up with his studies, Jeff thought. Evidently bas-ketball wasn't in his blood as it was in Jeff's. And Gil was good, the best on the team. He'd surely get on the varsity if he stayed.

Jeff shook his head. He compared himself with Gil. Gil was a brilliant basketball player. He handled him-self expertly on the court. He was good at set shots as well as lay-ups. He could break up plays better than anyone and was quick as lightning. He was everything a basketball player should be. Yet he wanted to quit because he couldn't keep up with his studies.

Why can't I be like Gil? thought Jeff. I'd give any-thing to be as good as he is.

But Gil was right. Jeff had the advantage when it came to studies.

The Saturday noon sun looked like the yolk of an egg amid the cottony shreds of clouds. A shiny black car stood at the curb. Jeff went to it.

"Hi, Dad," he said. "Been waiting long?"

"Hi, Son." Mr. Dooley's gray eyes warmed behind dark-rimmed glasses. He was wearing his usual dark gray suit, dark hat, and pastel-blue necktie. "No. I just got here," he said.

Mr. Dooley started the car and sent it cruising from the curb.

"Are you very hungry, Jeff?" he asked.

"Kind of. We had a pretty tough scrimmage."

"Can you go for another half hour or so without starving?"

Jeff shrugged.

"I guess so. Why?"

His father smiled.

"I'll show you in a few minutes."

The big car moved smoothly along the city streets. Jeff relaxed against the seat, wondering what his father was up to. They left the city limits and made some turns which looked familiar. In a little while the car came to a stop in the parking lot of the city airport.

"What're we doing here, Dad?" Jeff asked.

His father grinned.

"Come on. You'll see."

Mr. Dooley led Jeff across a walk and then through a gate. Five planes of various makes were parked near the edge of the huge runway. From the cabin of the fifth plane emerged a familiar figure. Jeff was surprised when he realized that it was Kevin, his older brother.

"What's Kevin doing here?" he asked.

"That's Kevin's plane," Mr. Dooley said. "Your

brother finally saved enough cash to buy himself a secondhand Aeronca Champion."

Jeff still didn't understand. He knew that Kevin, who was about eight years older than he, loved flying. But he and Jeff were very different. What could Jeff have to do with this?

"Hi, Jeff," said Kevin, his dark hair blowing all over his head, and a big happy smile on his handsome young face. "Look what your big brother's got."

Jeff admired the single-wing, red and yellow plane.

"Dad told me," he said. "It sure is a beauty."

Mr. Dooley put an arm around Jeff's shoulders.

"Kevin's arranged to have you take flying lessons, Jeff. What do you think of that?"

Jeff frowned.

"Me take flying lessons? Why? I never said I cared that much for flying."

His father smiled.

"I know, but flying and electronics go hand in hand, Jeff. It's the thing now. You have to think about what you're going to do when you get out of high school. And this is it. This is the ground floor. Kevin and I want to help you get started."

Jeff looked at his father. Suddenly he knew what this was all about. It was a plan—a very sly plan to take his interest away from basketball.

CHAPTER 2

"Would you like to come up for a few minutes, Jeff?" asked Kevin. "I'll let you take over the controls for a while."

Jeff met Kevin's eyes squarely. He wondered whether his father had put Kevin up to this. Kevin, himself, didn't care for basketball or any other sport except flying. He did some swimming, but flying was his uppermost interest. He had had a pilot's license since graduating from college three years ago, and had talked about buying a plane ever since. Jeff had flown with him many times and had liked it. But ground sports had always been more fun for him. Leave the flying for the birds, or for fellows like Kevin whose work tied in with aeronautics.

"What's the matter, Jeff?" said his father, interrupting his thoughts. "You're taking a long time to answer. Would you rather come back some other time?"

"No. I'd like to go up now." Jeff looked at Kevin. "Ready?"

Kevin smiled.

"I'm waiting for you, kid."

"Okay. Come on."

Kevin opened the compartment door beneath the wing. Jeff climbed in the rear seat and Kevin in front. Kevin closed the door, checked the instrument panel, and started the engine. The propeller kicked over. The engine sputtered, then suddenly burst into life. Kevin fed the plane more gas, turning it around slowly until it faced the long runway. Then he gunned the motor. The plane rolled down the runway. Jeff watched from the side window. Soon the runway dipped away. They were airborne.

They climbed high in a wide sweeping circle. Below them the earth became a colorful checkerboard. The freight cars stationed near the depot and the Diesel engine pulling a car along another track looked a lot like the miniature train set Jeff had put away in the basement.

They flew over Carson, a town so small that every one of its buildings could be seen from an altitude of five hundred feet. Jeff picked out his own home on Durston Street, Mike's Restaurant on the corner, and just across from it Rockwell's Drugstore. The sight from up high was always a thrill.

Kevin turned and smiled at him.

"Go ahead! Grab hold of the stick!"

Jeff could hardly believe his ears. Kevin had never allowed him to touch any of the controls.

"What do you want me to do?" he said.

"Just take the stick! Don't worry! I'll hang on to the stick in front just in case!"

Jeff grinned and grabbed the stick nervously. He held it rigid for a while, feeling it budge this way and that against the palm of his hand. Then he moved it cautiously to the right. The plane dipped slightly. Kevin turned around and smiled.

"How does it feel?"

"Good!"

"Now move it to the left! Easy!"

Jeff moved the stick to the left. The plane leveled off, dipped to the left. Then he brought the stick back to an upright position and the plane leveled off again.

Kevin looked around.

"You're doing all right, kid! How would you like to really learn to fly?"

Jeff shrugged.

"I think I would."

"There's nothing like it, Jeff! Nothing like it in the world!"

Jeff looked at his brother. Maybe there isn't for you, he thought. Kevin felt about flying as Jeff did about basketball. But there was a big difference between basketball and flying. Did you have fans shouting for you when you were in the air? Was the excitement the same when you sank in two points to tie the score just before the final horn blew?

That was the big difference. I like flying, thought Jeff. I like it a lot. But I like basketball better. In basketball you're playing *against* someone. You're playing to win. If you lose, okay. Somebody has to lose. If you win, you feel a thrill of satisfaction that lasts until the next time you play, and then it starts all over again.

"Okay," said Kevin. "I'll bring it in."

He landed the Champ gracefully, taxied it back to where it was before.

Mr. Dooley was in the hangar. He smiled broadly as Jeff walked in behind Kevin.

"Well, did Kevin let you take over the stick for a few minutes?" he asked.

Jeff nodded.

"Yep."

"Did you get a kick out of it?"

Jeff shrugged his shoulders.

"Yes."

"You'll get a bigger kick out of it when you can take up a plane by yourself," said Mr. Dooley. "Come in here. I want you to meet Mr. Tucker, the flight instructor."

Jeff followed his father into an office. A dark-haired girl wearing gold-rimmed glasses was sitting at a desk typing. At the far side of the office a tall man in a leather flying jacket was looking through a file drawer.

The girl stopped typing and looked up. Instantly her cheeks dimpled.

"Oh, hello, Mr. Dooley—Jeff. Kevin told me you were coming."

Jeff smiled as Kevin went over and took the girl's hands in his. Joan Haddock was Kevin's girl. Her father was Barney Haddock, manager of the airport. She looked at Jeff.

"Finally taking a real interest in flying, Jeff?"

"Well—I've always liked it," Jeff said. "Dad's just arranged to have me take flying lessons."

The man in the flying jacket came toward them. He

was at least six foot three, with reddish brown hair that looked hard to keep down, and blue eyes that were warm and friendly.

"Hiya," he said. Jeff detected a slight southern accent.

"Hi, Jim," said Mr. Dooley. "I want you to meet my younger son Jeff. Jeff, this is Jim Tucker. He hails from Texas, and has flown everything from kites to boxcars—so he tells me."

They shook hands. Jeff felt the strong firm grip of Jim Tucker's big hand and wondered if he'd ever played basketball.

"Glad to meet you, I'm sure," drawled Jim Tucker. "Any time you want to start your lessons, I'm ready."

"How about this afternoon?" said Mr. Dooley. "About three o'clock?"

"Fine by me," said the Texan. "How about you, Jeff?"

Jeff thought for a moment, then nodded. He had nothing to do this afternoon, anyway.

"Okay," he said.

Jim gave Jeff a book on flying and told him to read it.

After lunch, while waiting to return to the airport, Jeff thought how funny it was that his father had suggested he take flying lessons now. Why, it was almost winter. Freezing weather was due any time, and snow would start falling soon. What about his flying lessons then?

Kevin drove Jeff back to the airport, where they arrived a few minutes before three. With Jim Tucker was Barney Haddock, the manager, a tall broad-shoul-dered man with a wind-leathered face and clear blue eyes. He greeted Jeff with a friendly handshake and congratulated him on his decision to become a flier.

There wasn't much to the first lesson. Jim Tucker took Jeff up in a two-seater training plane and asked him questions. Did he know what made a plane fly? Did he know what made it climb, turn to the left and right? Jeff did know, since he had learned many of the fundamentals from his father and Kevin.

After the lesson, Kevin drove Jeff home.

"You'll learn it in no time," Mr. Dooley said in his loud happy manner at the supper table. "Why, I bet that within a month you'll be able to fly solo."

"If the weather stays nice I might," said Jeff.

"Let's hope it does," said Mr. Dooley. "The more flying you do the better. You'll be progressing then. But basketball! What is there about basketball that makes you want to go out in all kinds of weather to practice? Running up and down, back and forth, just to throw a ball through a net. It's for boys, Jeff, I ad-mit it. But not for boys like you."

Jeff looked up at his father. He felt a tightness in his chest.

"Dad! What do you mean? What kind of boy am I? What's different about me?"

His father's eyes turned on him sharply, then quickly softened.

"You know what I mean, Jeff," he said, lowering his voice. "You're young. Now is the time for you to buckle down and get an education. It isn't hard nowadays to decide what you want to be. What do you read in the headlines every day? Guided missiles. Satellites spinning around the world. Nuclear energy. They're all in front of you, waiting for you to take the plunge. Boys like you are scarce, worth their weight in gold. You see what I'm talking about, son, don't you?"

Jeff kept silent, his father's words searing his brain.

"I don't want you to be wasting away your youth on something that doesn't matter," said Mr. Dooley. "I want you to be like Kevin—like *me*." His voice rose impressively when he said "like *me*."

Then Jeff's mother spoke.

"Easy, dear. You may suggest a career for Jeff, but pushing him into it won't do any good."

"I'm *not* pushing him," said Mr. Dooley. "I'm only telling him what's best for him."

"Why don't you eat your supper before it gets cold," his wife said gently. "Go on, Jeff. Eat. It'll be two and a half years yet before you'll have to start thinking about guided missiles and flying satellites."

At school Monday afternoon, just as Jeff was heading for the gym to watch a scrub basketball game, someone called after him. He turned and saw the somber face of Mr. Gregory, the partly bald and squeamish-looking science teacher.

"Jeff, come here a minute, will you?"

Jeff turned and followed Mr. Gregory, reluctantly, into his room. Jeff didn't like Mr. Gregory, although he did respect his knowledge of the subjects he taught. Mr. Gregory seemed to have little use for sports. At least, Jeff didn't remember ever seeing him at any of the basketball games. Jeff hated to put his father in the same category with Mr. Gregory, but the two were very much alike in some ways. Jeff sighed briefly as he slumped into a seat.

Mr. Gregory cleared his throat and eyed Jeff for a moment before he started to speak.

"I hear you've been practicing basketball, Jeff."

"That's right," Jeff said.

Mr. Gregory cleared his throat again.

"Isn't it rather—well, I mean, don't you think you're making a mistake?"

"Mistake?" Jeff asked. "What do you mean, Mr. Gregory?"

Mr. Gregory smiled gently, and rubbed his nose and chin with a forefinger.

"Well, I've always been inclined to think rather highly of you, Jeff. I've known your father very well for a good many years, and your mother, too. Your father is one of the most talented electronics engineers in the country, and your brother Kevin is climbing fast in his field, too. Neither one of them—your father nor your brother—has ever wasted his time playing sports. They've used their energies to benefit science, which means to benefit mankind."

Jeff looked away. He felt the blood rush to his neck. He wanted to get up and run out. For crying out loud, he wasn't Kevin! He wasn't his father! Couldn't he live his own life?

Jeff swallowed. He controlled himself and looked up at Mr. Gregory without blinking.

"What have my marks been so far this year, Mr. Gregory?" he asked steadily.

Mr. Gregory lifted his shoulders gently.

"They're right up there, Jeff. Ninety-plus average. But they'll go down. Playing basketball will bring them down."

Jeff stood up. He felt his heart beating wildly against his ribs.

"I'll do my best to keep them up. Is that all you wanted to see me about, Mr. Gregory?"

Mr. Gregory nodded.

"That's all, Jeff."

"May I go now?"

"You may. But think about what I said. I meant it as a warning."

CHAPTER 3

JEFF met Gil Baker and Bruce Parker in the hall.

"Hi, guys," he said and looked at Gil. "We going to see you at practice tonight?"

"I think so," said Gil.

"Good. Glad you'll be there. With you gone we wouldn't amount to very much, Gil."

Gil smiled bashfully.

"Oh, I'm just lucky," he said.

"Golly," said Jeff. "I wish I was that lucky."

When Jeff told them about his talk with Mr. Gregory, Bruce said:

"Why doesn't he keep his nose out of this? It's a good thing he's not our principal. If he had his way we wouldn't have any sports at all."

Practice after school began with the usual warm-up shots, followed by lay-ups, set shots, and man-in-the-middle drills. Jeff worked hard. His lay-ups had improved considerably since the season started. He was weak with his set shots, though, usually throwing the ball either to the left or right of the basket. But he expected to improve his aim in time. In foul shooting he was on a par with Gil and the rest of the first stringers.

After practice Coach Stu Cochran announced that next week there would be two practice games.

"Brighton and Lincoln," he said. "Our scheduled league games begin the week after that. We're playing each team twice, which will give us a pretty full season. If we're good, we get into the play offs. But we have a lot of time to talk about that later. Okay, let's knock off."

A few moments later the locker room hummed with talk about the coming games with Brighton and Lincoln. Jeff was beginning to feel the usual pre-game excitement already. At last, after so much practice, there would be a real scrimmage.

When Jeff arrived home, his father was sitting in the living room reading the evening paper. As they greeted each other, Jeff felt the gray eyes look at him searchingly over the edge of the paper. He went to his room, hung up his coat and hat, then sat down on the edge of the bed. He was thinking of his father's eyes. He had seen disappointment in them. But why was that? Jeff wondered. Was it simply because he had played basketball that afternoon?

Later a soft voice called him.

"Jeff."

Jeff looked up and saw his father in the doorway. Those eyes were brighter now. They were kind. But Jeff knew his father was a stubborn man. He turned away and looked out the window at the lone bare tree bending under the pressure of the wind, and the pink quilt blanket whipping like a huge pennant on the clothesline.

"Were you practicing basketball this afternoon?" Mr. Dooley asked.

Jeff nodded.

Mr. Dooley came into the room. His voice went on softly.

"What's the matter, Jeff? Don't you want to talk to me?"

Jeff turned his head part way. What an awkward moment this was.

"It isn't that, Dad. It's—well, I know what you're thinking."

His father sighed.

"Yes, I suppose you do. But it makes no difference, does it? I'm an old codger who never cared for sports. I'm from the old school. All I can think about is cramming your mind with knowledge. Is that what you're thinking?"

"Please, Dad. Don't say that."

"But it's the truth, isn't it?"

Jeff didn't answer. It was hard to say, "Yes, that's the truth," when he knew it would only hurt his father.

Jeff's mind worked desperately. He heard his father's footsteps leaving the room.

"Dad—wait."

His father paused at the threshold and looked back. "Yes, Jeff?"

"Do you want me actually to give up basketball, Dad? Would that make you happy?"

"You know I think flying is more important, Jeff. I'd like to see you devote more time to that."

"Give me a little time to think it over, will you?" Jeff said. "Two or three weeks?"

His father smiled. His eyes crinkled.

"Okay, Jeff. Do you want to talk to Kevin about it? I'll tell him if—"

"No, thanks, Dad. I'll have to figure this out by myself."

"Don't you like flying?"

"Sure I do, Dad. It isn't that. It's—well, can I think about it?"

"All right, son. Think about it. That's fair enough." Mr. Dooley came over to his son and patted him affectionately on the back. "I want you to do the right thing, Jeff. That's why I want to help."

Jeff wondered—did his dad know what the right thing was?

On the night of the first scrimmage with Brighton, the Carson Central jayvees were on the court twenty minutes before game time. Wearing black and orange satin jackets, the team trotted out in single file. The team manager pulled out four balls from a canvas bag and tossed them out on the floor. They were picked up by eager hands, bounced, and then sailed through the air toward the baskets.

All day long Jeff had thought about tonight's game, but also of the promise he had made to his father. He was confused and worried. He found now that by running around the court, shooting baskets, and concentrating on the game ahead, he could relax a bit.

School kids and adults began filing in to the seats that lined the two wider sides of the gym. Jeff felt the pre-game tension growing inside him, and now he thought of nothing else. He watched the Brighton jayvees in their warm-up shots. Their center was a six-footer, but the rest of the team seemed to match the Carson players almost man for man.

Finally the coaches called their squads off the court. Coach Cochran stood in a circle with his boys. His wide shoulders fitted snugly in his dark suit coat. His serious blue eyes flicked to each of his men as he talked.

"Even though this is a non-league game, I expect you to do your best out there. Try to make every move count. The starting line-up will be Gil Baker at left forward, Jeff Dooley right forward, Lee Mattoon at center, Bruce Parker at right guard, and Eddie Russell at left guard. Okay. Get in there and hustle."

Jeff's excitement knew no bounds. The coach had selected him over Eric Wilson and Bill Godell. He knew it didn't mean that he was definitely a first stringer—he would have to prove his worth in this game, and the next, and the next after that. . . .

The buzzer sounded. Both teams waited on the court while Lee Mattoon, Carson's captain, and the Brighton captain chose their baskets and went over some of the court rules. Then the referee blew his whistle.

The men got into position, shook hands, checked the numbers on their backs, and readied for the toss-up between the two centers.

Up went the ball. Lee shot up with it, tapped the ball to his left. Gil swooped in, caught it, passed to Bruce. Bruce dribbled across the center line and shot an overhand pass to Jeff. A Brighton player sprang up, knocking the ball out of bounds. Jeff took it out, bounce-passed to Gil. Gil dribbled through a huddle of players and leaped for a lay-up.

Two points!

Brighton took the ball out of bounds. They worked it across the court toward their basket. Jeff dove forward to intercept a pass and caught it just as a Brighton player got his hands on the ball. They fought for control of the ball until the frantic screeching of the referee's whistle stopped them. His two thumbs jerked upward.

Jeff out-jumped his opponent and tapped the ball to Bruce. Bruce passed quickly to Eddie Russell. Eddie dribbled hard down court as two Brighton players shot after him. Eddie stopped, feinted a throw to Jeff, and passed to Bruce. Bruce started to dribble, then hung on the ball. The Brighton players had the area under the basket well protected, preventing any dribbling in.

Bruce passed, and for a while the ball was zipped back and forth among the Carson players. When Jeff had possession of the ball, a Brighton man swept in, trying to knock it from his hands. Jeff feinted to the left, pulled his man off guard, and burst in for a fast break. He went up under the basket, pushing the ball up with one hand. The ball riffled through the net for two more points.

There was a deafening roar from the Carson fans. Carson had begun to move. They sank two more baskets to make the score 8–0. Then a Brighton forward, a young, husky lad with glasses, dribbled the ball across the center line through the Carson squad and dumped in a perfect lay-up.

The score now made the Brighton jayvees play harder, and by the end of the first quarter the score was Carson–14, Brighton–10.

Eric started in place of Jeff in the second period. He scored twice on sets, and sank a free throw. But he also fouled twice and Cochran took him out. Jeff went back in until the half-time buzzer sounded. Carson was still in the lead, 18–16.

"Watch Davis, the kid with the glasses," said Coach Cochran to his boys in the locker room. "He's hitting like a hawk, but only from the right side of the basket. He's your man, Jeff. Cover him well."

The second half was begun with the same starting line-up that had started the game. Jeff played Davis, the Brighton forward, closely. Once Jeff intercepted a pass and scored with a quick set shot. The cheers were loud proof that he had executed a dazzling play. Then Lee sank a long shot from the far edge of the ten-second line, just before the third quarter ended, pulling them out of a tie.

In the fourth quarter, Brighton powered their way to three baskets in machine-gun style. Lee called time.

"Come on, you guys. Let's stop 'em," he said, toweling the sweat from his face. "They're four points ahead. Let's get going!"

The time-in buzzer sounded. Carson tossed in the ball from out of bounds. Bruce was called on traveling. Brighton took it out, streaked like a flash down the court. Jeff sprinted after the dribbler. He reached out for the bouncing ball. Suddenly the Brighton man stopped, got set, and shot. The ball bounded off the rim of the basket. Jeff leaped, caught the rebound, and back-passed to Eddie. Eddie passed to Gil, who bolted up court, and scored with a lay-up.

Jeff glanced up. The red dots on the scoreboard flashed HOME–30, VISITORS–32. According to the clock, there were only three minutes and twenty seconds to go.

Carson fouled and Brighton made both free shots. Then Jeff sank a long one and Lee dumped in a left-hand pivot shot that tied the score. With thirty seconds left Carson fouled again and Brighton got one free throw. Brighton made it, and pandemonium broke loose.

A few seconds later the end-of-game buzzer sounded. Carson suffered its first defeat of the season, 35–34.

CHAPTER 4

THE LIVING-ROOM lights were on when Jeff got home. He pushed open the front door. Kevin and his mother were up watching television.

"Hi," he said. "Where's Dad? In bed?" He probably didn't want to stay up to wait for me, thought Jeff. Sore because I played basketball.

"No. He's still at the office," said Kevin. "He's working on something important."

Jeff yanked off his coat. Something important. That meant that his father was preparing another secret project to be put up for government bid. Something to do with missiles, or turbo-jets, or maybe even one of those rockets for sending aloft a baby moon.

"Did you win or lose?" asked Kevin. "You don't look especially happy."

"We lost by one point," said Jeff. "Thirty-five to thirty-four."

"Did you play?"

"Yes. I started, and played most of the game."

"Good."

Jeff glanced sharply at Kevin. Did Kevin mean it?

27

Was he really interested? Or had he just said that to make Jeff feel better?

"Hungry?" asked Mrs. Dooley. There was a faint twinkle in her brown eyes. Jeff knew his mother was the only member of the family who did not resent his playing basketball.

"A little, Mom," said Jeff. "I'd love a cheese sandwich and a cup of hot cocoa."

"Cheese sandwich and hot cocoa coming up," she said and went into the kitchen.

Jeff was ready to go to bed when his dad came home.

"Hello, everybody," greeted Mr. Dooley. His face was beaming with triumph. He hummed as he unbuttoned his coat and draped it over a chair, laid his hat on top of it, and then excitedly rubbed his palms together.

"You just finished the best project the laboratory has ever produced," said Kevin soberly.

"You guessed it," said Mr. Dooley. "I wish it wasn't top secret. I'd tell you all about it, that's how certain I am of its success. I think it's the best thing that ever came out of Dunnigan. If it goes over—and I'm willing to bet that it will—it will draw a bigger contract than any we've had since the introduction of television."

"I hope you're right," said Kevin.

Mr. Dooley looked at Jeff. The glow of triumph was burning in his eyes.

"I wish you were in it with me now, Jeff. Kevin knows what I'm talking about. He can feel the enthusiasm I feel, because we work together under the same room. He's not working with me on this particular project, and I'm sorry, in a way, that he isn't. But he's working on something equally important."

"Jet planes," said Kevin. "Nothing secret about that. The only things secret are the details, and I haven't got a photographic memory anyway."

"I'm glad you've got it done, Dad," Jeff said. "Guess I'd better turn in, now."

Not a word from his father about how the game had turned out. Or whether he had played.

Jeff felt bitter disappointment as he climbed into bed and pulled the covers over him.

During science period the next day, Mr. Gregory announced that he was preparing a test which he would give the class on Thursday. It would be a tough one, he added emphatically, looking hard at Jeff and Gil Baker.

The jayvees practiced that evening, finishing with a twenty-minute scrimmage. Jeff played the first ten minutes with the first stringers, then went with the second team. Coach Cochran had Bill Godell and Eric Wilson team up as forwards with Lee, Bruce, and Eddie. Eric played opposite Jeff. He stole the ball from Jeff once and dribbled the full length of the court for a basket. Another time he intercepted a pass intended for Jeff, and passed it to Lee who dribbled down court and dumped in a bucket.

Bill Godell was holding his own, too. He attempted a couple of set shots from the free-throw line and sank both. He also tried several one-hand push ups. They were all perfect.

Jeff watched and remembered both players' actions. They were good, no doubt about it. He had to do his best to keep a notch ahead of them.

At supper that evening Mr. Dooley asked a question which Jeff had been expecting since Sunday.

"How are you doing with that book on flying that Jim Tucker gave you, Jeff?"

Jeff felt the blood rush to his face. "I've read part of it," he said.

"What! I thought you'd have it all finished by now," Mr. Dooley said. "Haven't you had enough time?"

"Well—with studies to do, I guess not." Jeff kept his eyes on his plate.

"Are you taking your second flying lesson Saturday?"

"I expect to."

"You haven't made up your mind yet, I suppose?" Mr. Dooley asked.

Jeff knew what he meant.

"No, Dad. I haven't. Not yet."

There was a strained silence for a moment. Jeff suddenly didn't feel like eating, but he didn't want to ask permission to leave the table—that would only start an argument between his mom and dad.

"When's your next game?" Kevin said, breaking the awkward stillness.

"Tomorrow," said Jeff.

Mr. Dooley glanced at Kevin, and it was perfectly clear from his expression that he didn't want the subject of basketball brought up.

Kevin took a last mouthful and pushed his plate aside.

"Excuse me," he said and left the table.

A little while later Kevin put on his coat and hat and left the house. Jeff figured Kevin had a date with Joan and was probably going to take her to a movie.

Jeff went to his room to study for the science test. He felt sure that Mr. Gregory was going to show no mercy for anyone, especially not for a couple of basketball players.

In the morning, each student in the science class received two sheets of questions, and for forty minutes the room was absolutely still. Once a pencil dropped on the floor and rolled a little way. Feet scuffled, and a seat squeaked as someone changed position, but those were the only audible sounds in the room.

Jeff felt hot, and twice had to mop his brow. The questions were tough, all right. Mr. Gregory had shown no mercy.

Finally time was up. The students passed their papers to the front desks and Mr. Gregory gathered them up. He looked at Jeff and Gil as he straightened out the papers in his hands. This expression was challenging.

"How do you think you made out, Gil?" Jeff asked as the two boys walked out of the room to their next class.

"I don't know," said Gil. "I'll be lucky to get sixty. I think he gave us a real hard one just to pull our marks down."

"I think so, too," said Jeff. "He hates sports so much he'd like to keep us from playing even if he has to give us a test every day."

"How do you think you did?"

Jeff shrugged.

"I studied hard last night. Probably about seventy-five or eighty."

They turned the corner in the hall.

"By the way, have you decided what you're going to do, Gil?"

"You mean about quitting?"

"Yes."

"I think I will quit. I want to go to college, and the only way my folks can afford it is for me to get a couple of scholarships."

"But you can get athletic scholarships," said Jeff.

"With low marks?" Gil shook his head. "I doubt it."

"I guess you're right," said Jeff.

Jeff didn't have to worry about scholarships. His folks could afford to pay his way through four years of college, or even six. But he had heard of many students paying a part of their way by working during the summer vacations. He probably would, too.

Gil's situation was different. His father was a salt miner with a very modest income. Gil was the oldest of five children. He wanted to go to college—to help himself, and to enable him to help relieve the heavy financial burden of raising his brothers and sisters.

Jeff couldn't blame Gil. He would do the same in his shoes.

"I'll play against Lincoln," said Gil, "And that'll be it. Then I'll tell Coach Cochran I'm done. Anyway, I guess he's expecting it."

"You're taking more than four subjects, aren't you, Gil?"

"Six, besides choir."

"Can't you drop one or two?"

"No. I'd rather drop out of basketball."

Jeff shook his head.

"Boy, I can't understand that."

"Understand what?"

"A good basketball player like you wanting to drop basketball. Why, I bet before the season's over Coach Wilkins'll snatch you up for the varsity."

A smile brushed Gil's lips.

"It doesn't make any difference, Jeff. A guy can only play basketball so long, you know. Then there's the chance of getting hurt so bad you can't play any more. Then what?"

Jeff shrugged.

"You can get hurt doing anything, Gil. Even walking along these halls, or down the steps."

They paused at the door of their next classroom.

"How's the flying coming?" Gil asked, ignoring Jeff's remark.

Jeff raised his eyebrows.

"Oh, you've heard?"

Gil nodded.

"Oh, sure. News travels fast along the grapevine.

How come you've decided to take up flying now—in the wintertime?"

Jeff hesitated. He didn't know whether to tell Gil the truth or not. So long as he could keep his father's name out of it, he would.

"My brother Kevin bought a plane," he said. "He's helping me to learn. It shouldn't take me too long."

"You're lucky," said Gil. "I wish I had that chance. I'm crazy about flying, too."

Jeff looked at him. Gil turned and walked into the room, Jeff behind him. We're some pair, thought Jeff. He doesn't like what he can do, and I don't especially like what I can do. But I like what he doesn't, and he likes what I don't. What a couple of corkers we are!

CHAPTER 5

THE GAME against Lincoln High stimulated a lot of interest. The Lincoln team had been the playoffs champions the year before.

Jeff was happy that Coach Cochran had scheduled a non-league game with them. Lincoln, a tougher team than Brighton, would provide a test of Carson's strength before their regular league games started.

However, Eddie Russell and some of the others had different opinions.

"Those guys'll swamp us," said Eddie. "They'll take us like Grant took Richmond."

"We'll look like a bunch of phonies out there," said Bruce Parker.

"Are you giving up already?" said Jeff. "So what if they're tough? That just ought to make us play harder."

"That's right," said Bill Godell. "They don't put any more men on the floor than we do."

"Their jayvees are almost like our varsity," argued Bruce.

"Oh, cut it out," said big Lee Mattoon, towering

over all of them. "Where's your guts? We'll play 'em, and we'll take 'em."

Jeff smiled.

"That's the way to talk, Lee."

There were only a few available spaces left for spectators by the time the game started at six-thirty. The Lincoln Leopards had colorful uniforms—yellow and black with the picture of a leopard on the front of the jerseys. What Bruce had said about them seemed very true. They looked the size of Carson Central's varsity.

Coach Cochran called the squad together.

"Don't let those fellows scare you," he said. "Some of them are bigger than you are but slow on their feet. Do a lot of running. Wear 'em down. Eric Wilson and Gil Baker will start at forward, Lee at center, Bruce Parker and Bill Godell at guard. One more word: Watch your fouls. If and when you do make one, don't sulk or get mad about it. It happens to everybody. Raise your hand to show the scorekeeper who made the foul. Okay. Good luck."

The five starters walked out onto the court; the rest of the players sat down. Jeff was very disappointed. He'd felt sure he was going to start.

A few seconds later Eddie nudged him and said:

"Relax. You'll have your arm chewed off at the rate you're going."

Boy! he thought. He'd been biting his nails and didn't know it.

Hardly a minute had gone by and the Leopards were ahead, 6–0. Carson was doing a lot of running, but the strategy was working in reverse. The Leopards had the ball most of the time, and Carson was chasing them.

Then Eric caught a pass in the free-throw lane and dribbled toward the corner of the court. He stopped, leaped, and hooked a shot at the basket. The ball struck the rim, hit the backboard, and fell through the net.

The Carson fans cheered lustily, and their cheers were heightened by the loud shouts of the jayvees' cheerleaders who were sitting on the bottom row of the bleachers, directly opposite the Carson players.

Lincoln took the ball out and worked it swiftly down the court. Carson swooped on them like a flock of sparrows attacking a hawk. Lincoln bullet-passed back and forth across the court, trying to get closer to their basket, but each move was stopped by a quick-moving Carson player. They were hustling now, on the go every second.

Then a Lincoln player feinted a throw for the basket, whisked away from his guard, and charged for the hoop. Just as he leaped Eric bolted in, and both collapsed on the floor in a heap. The ball rolled out of bounds under the basket. The whistle screeched.

The referee held up his hands, palms frontward, indicating charging. He lifted two fingers and pointed at Eric.

The two players got up. Eric bowed his head—the fall had mussed his groomed hair—and lifted his arm to show that he was the offender.

The Lincoln player bounced the ball on the floor in

front of him, then got set and threw his foul shot. The ball arched beautifully and fluttered through the net without touching the rim. The Lincoln fans responded with a loud cheer.

"Ball in play," announced the referee as he handed the ball to the Lincoln player for his second shot.

This time the ball fell short. It hit the rim, bounded up, arched downward. Both teams leaped for it. Jeff saw Eric right in the middle of the play, fighting like a bantam rooster, full of spunk, nerve, spirit. Eric's good, thought Jeff. He's in every play. Maybe I'll be lucky to get in this time at all.

The first quarter ended. The colored electric balls on the scoreboard read: HOME–4, VISITORS–9.

"All right, Jeff," said Coach Cochran. "Take Eric's place. Eddie, replace Bill. Don't forget, keep 'em running. They only scored once during those last three minutes."

Jeff was pleased. He shook hands with his man, Number 12. They were about the same height and build. Jeff recalled that Number 12 had scored four points against Eric. He favored a one-hand push-up shot, and the two times he'd scored, the ball had swished through the hoop touching nothing but the net.

Carson took the ball out of bounds. Lee passed to Jeff, Jeff to Eddie. Eddie dribbled fast toward the basket, but stopped quickly as two Lincoln men swooped in front of him. He pivoted, and passed back to Lee. Lee looked around for someone to pass to, then directed his aim to the basket. Just as he leaped to shoot, Jeff rushed down the side line. Instead of the ball's arching for the basket, it sailed like a bullet at Jeff. Jeff caught it, leaped, and dumped in a perfect lay-up for two points.

"Nice going," Lee said to Jeff as Jeff came running up beside him.

"You, too." Jeff smiled.

Lincoln took the ball out and moved it to the front court in quick short passes. Number 12 caught it and dribbled in toward the basket. Jeff got in front of him, tried to snatch away the bouncing ball. Number 12 stopped, pivoted, and set his eye on the basket. Jeff charged in. "Shoot," he yelled. Number 12 shot. His aim was off. The ball struck the outer rim of the hoop and bounded off.

A dozen hands shot up to intercept the rebound. A Lincoln player took it on his finger tips, leaped. The ball struck the backboard, and dropped over the other side of the basket. Again white arms stretched high, and eager fingers waited to snatch the ball.

Two big hands pulled it down. For a moment it was out of sight. Then big Lee Mattoon straightened to his full height, holding the ball aloft and away from Lincoln players who were fighting to nab it from him.

"Here!" said Jeff.

Lee snapped an over-the-shoulder pass. The ball glanced off the finger tips of a Lincoln man and bounced across the floor. Jeff and two Lincoln men raced after it. Jeff got it, dribbled across the free-throw line, and shot up in front of the basket, the ball high over his head. His feet hit the floor hard and he plunged against the protective canvas mat, just as cheers burst forth from the Carson side of the court.

A few seconds later Jeff intercepted a pass intended for Eddie's man, and passed the ball to Gil who stood free in the back corner. Gil worked the ball up quickly. He dribbled across the center line, then shot a quick pass to Lee. Lee feinted a shot at the basket, then back-passed to Gil who came running up behind him. Gil took the ball and charged in for a lay-up. A Lincoln man struck his arm as he scored a perfect basket.

Shrie-e-e-e-k! A foul!

But the score counted, and once again the Carson cheerleaders echoed their praises, for Carson was forging ahead now, 10–9.

"One shot," said the referee.

The gym grew silent as Gil took his place at the free-throw line. He took the ball, held it calmly in front of him. He shot it from his chest. The ball looped, struck the back side of the rim, wobbled through.

Score: Carson–11, Lincoln–9.

"Time!" shouted the Lincoln captain, holding the tip of his right hand against the palm of his left in a T shape.

The referee blew his whistle.

"We've got them on the run," Bruce said as the squad huddled together. "Nice shooting, Gil."

"Thanks," Gil said. "Jeff's done some nice shooting, too."

Jeff smiled. This was what he liked, this was the excitement he loved more than anything else. Maybe that was why he was doing so well. The more he played, the more fun it was and the more he could put into it. I wonder, Jeff thought, if Gil ever looked at basketball that way.

"You know what they want those two minutes for, don't you?" said Coach Cochran.

"Sure," said Bruce. "They need the rest."

"So do I," gasped Lee. His sweaty face broke into a wide grin. The others laughed.

"Okay," said the coach. "Rest up. We've only a couple more minutes to go in this quarter, anyway. Jim Barclay go in for Lee."

"Oh, I can play, coach. I was only kidding," Lee protested.

"Kidding, heck," said the coach. "I want to see what Jim can do, anyway."

Time-in was called. Lincoln took the ball from out of bounds and in less than twenty seconds scored a basket, then dumped in two more in rapid succession. Gil pulled two free throws on a personal foul. He made the first shot, failed the second, and then the half was over.

The electric scoreboard read: HOME–12, VISI-TORS–15.

Jeff started the second half. Before a minute was up he scored a lay-up with the help of Gil Baker who shot him a short pass from the free-throw line. Then Lincoln got going and sank baskets from all over their half of the court. They were ahead by ten points when the third period ended.

"We've got to stop them this last quarter," said Coach Cochran. "Jeff, I'll let you and Gil rest for a few minutes. Eric and Sam, you boys go in. Keep them on the run. If they're going to shoot, don't give them a chance to aim. Then they'll shoot fast and miss. Okay. Let's see the old fight."

Coach Cochran's suggestion worked. Carson made Lincoln hurry their shots, and the results were many misses. But Lee, the tallest man to take the rebounds, was not able alone to outplay the three or four tall boys on the Lincoln team. Eric Wilson and Sam Bullick were too short to nab the rebounds, so with four minutes to play Coach Cochran put Jeff and Gil in again and almost instantly the picture changed.

Gil caught two rebounds himself within seconds, and the Lincoln players found themselves plowing through a field of molasses. One long shot was successful, but it was the only one. Carson, however, needed baskets to close the gap in the score and to win.

The gap narrowed. But time ran out with Carson trailing by four points. Score: Carson–29, Lincoln–33.

Jeff ran down the steps to the locker room still out of breath. They had lost, but losing by four points to last year's playoffs champions was no disgrace. Anyway, this was a game that didn't count in the official scorebook . . . Though in Jeff's book it did. It counted an awful lot.

CHAPTER 6

Mr. Dooley drove Jeff to the airport for Jeff's second flying lesson. The Saturday morning sun was a bright brassy ball that felt like a hot pad against Jeff's thigh as it blazed through the closed window of the car. But once the car was parked and they got out, the air had a bitter sting.

Jeff wondered how many more times he'd be coming here for lessons. There was bound to be snow eventually; it was due any time.

Mr. Dooley led the way to the office facing the long runway. Jeff heard the roar of a plane overhead. He looked up and recognized a Stinson Station Wagon. Its motor cut and its left wing dipped. It banked, came in for a landing, and parked beside one of the other planes grouped off the runway. The door opened and two men climbed out. One was Jim Tucker. Jeff would recognize that rangy body and easygoing stride anywhere.

"Hi, Mr. Dooley. Hi, Jeff," Jim said as he came up to them, grinning broadly. "All ready to go with another lesson in air power?"

Jeff smiled and nodded.

"All ready," he said.

"Be with you in a minute," Jim said.

"Did you study your flying book pretty well?" Mr. Dooley asked again as Jim and the other man walked off toward the office. "Do you think you know most of the answers?"

Jeff shook his head. "There's a lot of technical stuff in that book, Dad. I can't learn it all in a couple of weeks."

"I know, I know," agreed his father. "I just want you to be a good pupil, Jeff." He put a cigar in his mouth and lit it with a match. "Try to get all you can out of this," he continued, whipping out the match flame and throwing the burnt match aside. "We've got to take advantage of this good weather. I don't want you to be going up when the weather gets bad."

Jeff looked at his father, at the thin lines edging those sharp gray eyes that were now directed anxiously toward the office door. His father had been thinking about the weather, too.

Soon Jim Tucker came out.

"You can wait inside the office if you like, Mr. Dooley," he said.

"Thanks, Jim. I will."

Jeff went with Jim to an Aeronca similar to Kevin's, the same one they had used the week before. Jim started the engine. He taxied the plane down to the end of the runway, then gave it full throttle. The single-wing plane sped down the smooth runway, then shot into the air.

They climbed up to a thousand feet, and Jim began

asking Jeff questions—finding out what Jeff had learned, how much he had studied. Jeff gave his answers frankly. And then Jim let him take over the controls, at the same time keeping his own hand on the stick to correct any error Jeff might make.

"You're doing fine, kid," Jim said to him from the rear seat. "One thing, though. You're yanking the stick too quick when you want to change your course. Do it easy. Hang on to the stick light now and feel how I do it."

Jeff did, and noticed how easily and smoothly Jim Tucker banked the plane.

Time passed swiftly. Jeff found that he had enjoyed the half hour of instructive flying and wished he could have stayed up with Jim longer. He thought about it on his way home. He noticed something else, too. Not once did his father ask him about basketball.

That afternoon he walked over to Lee Mattoon's house, where he found Lee and Eddie Russell watching a pro basketball game on television between the Minneapolis Lakers and the Syracuse Nats.

"Did you take a flying lesson this morning?" Eddie asked. He was sitting on an easy chair, his legs sprawled out in front of him.

Jeff nodded.

"Cold, wasn't it?"

"Not in the plane," replied Jeff.

Lee looked at him curiously.

"Aren't you pretty young to be a flier?"

"There's lots of kids younger than I am who fly," said Jeff. He began to feel uneasy.

"Are you going to take lessons all winter?" asked Eddie. "Even when it snows?"

Jeff pursed his lips.

"A little snow won't matter much. Only when it gets deep I guess I can't go up."

Eddie crossed his feet.

"Me and the guys were talking about you the other day, Jeff. We couldn't understand why you'd decided to take up flying."

Jeff had half expected this.

"What's so funny about it?" he said.

Eddie spread his palms.

"Just when basketball season starts, you ups and starts taking flying lessons. Funny coincidence, that's all."

Jeff tightened his lips. He didn't answer.

"You guys want some cookies and milk?" Lee asked.

"Sure," said Eddie. "I'm not in training."

"You, Jeff?"

"Yeah. I'll have some."

Jeff munched quietly on the cookies. The conversation shifted to Gil Baker.

"He played his last game against Lincoln," Lee said. "He's through. We're going to miss him plenty. He was tops."

"Jeff should take his place on the first string," Eddie said. "He's got it all over Eric."

"Thanks, Eddie," said Jeff. "But Eric's doing all right. He's got a good eye."

"For set shots, sure," Eddie said. "But for all around

playing you've got it all over him. He's too stiff from the shoulders up—too worried about getting that beautiful hair of his mussed."

"He's a crowd pleaser," Lee said. "Even the coach knows that. I think you've got it made, Jeff."

"Time will tell," Jeff replied.

He didn't tell them that he was riding the fence, too. That he might decide to drop basketball if he found it was a waste of time for him. He could sit on the bench, play only occasionally and still be satisfied, if his father didn't mind. Anyway, at the moment, he wanted to play regularly. He had to prove first to himself that he was valuable to the team. And then he had to prove it to his father, if that was at all possible.

Minneapolis took the Nats, 101–98. Jeff left, wishing he might have a chance to see a professional basketball game some day. But since his father and Kevin both disliked sports, he doubted that day would ever come.

Jeff wasn't surprised, when, the following day, Kevin asked him if he'd like to go flying.

"The weather's nice," said Kevin. "You can put in a half hour or so of training and it won't cost you a cent."

Kevin's smile was contagious. He boxed playfully with Jeff. Jeff put up a guard and retaliated with body blows that Kevin stopped with the swift cat-like movements of a real fighter. They clinched, and untangled.

Jeff shook his head.

"I don't get it, Kevin," he said. "You're tall, well

built. You're fast on your feet. You could've played any sport you wanted to and been good at it. Yet you didn't go out for any."

The smile on Kevin's face and the warmth in his eyes faded slightly.

"I swim a lot, remember. Also, I'm going to be the world's greatest scientist, second to none." He laughed. "Go on. Get into your duds."

Jeff went to his room, put on his jacket and a hat. Seconds later Kevin appeared from his room, similarly dressed. They both kissed their mother and walked out the kitchen door.

In the car Kevin asked Jeff:

"What do you think about flying? Think you'll stick to it?"

The question took Jeff by surprise.

"I like it," he said.

"But will you stick to it?"

Jeff thought a moment.

"I think I will, now that I've started. But I can't say for sure. For crying out loud, Kevin, I just started taking lessons."

"I know, Jeff," said Kevin. "I just wondered how it appealed to you now. Whether it was getting into your blood a little. You know."

"It probably has a little," admitted Jeff.

"It isn't just the flying part of it either," said Kevin. "Matter of fact, flying is just a small factor in what the future holds in store. It's guys like Dad and the others working at Dunnigan and similar laboratories, who will make the big changes that are bound to come.

You've seen what Russia has done. That's why we've got to concentrate on building up a strong force of young scientists. That force has to be led by guys like you, Jeff. And Gil Baker. Gil's doing the right thing to drop sports and concentrate on his studies."

Jeff was surprised.

"You've heard about Gil?"

"Sure. I was in Mike's Restaurant last night. Some of your cronies were in there and I heard them talking about it. They sounded grim, but Gil really shouldn't be criticized too severely. He realized he had to make a choice and made it, probably thinking that what he is going to be getting will be somewhat more worth while than a few extra points in a basketball game."

"Maybe you're right, Kevin," said Jeff. "But Gil is different from me. He doesn't care for basketball."

"But he was the best player on the team; at least, that's what those boys were saying."

"He was the best."

"But he didn't care for basketball?" Kevin's brows knitted together. "Yes, I guess that's possible. In a way he's a lot luckier than you are, Jeff, isn't he? He won't be hurt by not playing."

"That's right," said Jeff softly.

They arrived at the airport. Jeff helped Kevin pull the Champ out of the tiny hangar. The air was nippy. A breeze brushed Jeff's cheeks like a cold feather, riffled his trousers. Overhead the sky was bleak and overcast.

They pulled the plane onto the runway. Kevin and Jeff climbed in, Jeff in the rear seat. Kevin started the

engine, cracked the throttle, and let it run a few minutes to warm up.

Jeff leaned forward, looked over Kevin's shoulder
at the gas gauge.

"Are you going to gas it up?" he asked.

Kevin checked the gas.

"We're all right," he said confidently. "There's always a good supply of gas in a tank, even when it
shows low. In this case there's enough for about
twenty-five to thirty minutes."

Jeff sat back and relaxed. Kevin taxied down to the
end of the runway, let the engine idle a few more
seconds, then gently pushed the throttle forward. The
plane gathered speed as it rolled down the runway.
Its tail lifted. A moment later the nose raised and the
plane was airborne.

Kevin climbed to seven hundred feet. Jeff wiped
the fogged window beside him and looked down at
the city of Carson. Moments later they were cruising
over woods and fields, the green and reddish brown
colors forming a quilted pattern that touched Jeff's
heart.

He knew, quite definitely, that he liked flying. Perhaps when he grew older and graduated from high
school and then college, flying might become a part
of his career as his father was hoping. But the basketball question was still undetermined.

He realized how the sudden thought of basketball
made his heart do a flip. Instantly he saw, in a sort of
dream, a ball passing around a court, players dribbling and running, set shots and lay-ups sinking

through a net, and the flash of sweating bodies and flipping wrists. And all at once Jeff knew, with a certainty, that basketball was the love of his life now. Maybe later, when he was older, he might feel different. But now—today, tomorrow, and the next day—he wanted to play basketball more than anything else.

But what of his father? Should he hurt his father's feelings to satisfy his desire to play basketball?

A sudden coughing sound of the motor brought Jeff back to reality. He jerked forward in his seat and stared at the gas gauge. It showed almost empty.

And then the motor went dead. The only sound was the wind whistling against the wings of the plane.

"Kevin!" Jeff shouted. "What's happened?"

"I'm not sure," Kevin said. "Sounds like we're out of gas. But we can't be. The gauge still shows that there's some left."

Jeff's heart pounded as he leaned forward, tightly gripping Kevin's seat.

Kevin nosed the plane down in a glide to maintain air speed as long as possible.

"We'll never reach the airport," he said. "I've got to set it down in one of those fields ahead—and just hope that the one I pick won't be plowed so we'd ground loop."

Jeff felt sweat rise on his forehead. Kevin slid open the fogged window beside him and looked out. The frigid wind refreshed Jeff's face, but it did not cool the fear that had him in its grip. Kevin closed the window again.

What was going to happen now? Would they land

on a plowed field as Kevin said they might? What about the trees below, and the electric wires? Would Kevin be able to avoid these obstructions?

The altimeter needle was turning back rapidly. Five hundred feet . . . four fifty . . . four hundred . . . three fifty . . .

"There's a green pasture field up ahead," Kevin said, "but we'll never make it."

"Look! To the right of us! The field next to the road!" Jeff had spotted it from the right window.

Kevin dipped the plane to the right.

"The one with a barn near the road?"

"Yes!"

"It looks bumpy and rough," Kevin observed. "Say a prayer, Jeff and close your eyes!"

Jeff murmured a prayer, but he couldn't close his eyes. He had to see what was happening.

The plane was falling fast. The silence inside the cabin, with only the eerie whine of the wind outside, was deadly. It would be only a few seconds now, thought Jeff. Only a few . . .

And then the landing gear hit. There was a loud protesting report as every joint of the plane reacted under the impact. Jeff, even with the safety belt strapped around him, felt his head strike the back of the front seat. Sparkles flashed like fireflies in front of his eyes. He was tossed about like the ball inside a bell, and he was unable to stop.

CHAPTER 7

JEFF CONTROLLED HIMSELF. He did not scream. It seemed as if the terrible rocking would never stop. He shut his eyes and waited.

His mind was still reeling when he heard a familiar voice close beside him:

"Jeff, are you all right?"

Jeff opened his eyes, looked directly into the brown worried eyes of his brother.

"I guess so," he said. The front of his head ached. He put his hand where the pain was, and felt a lump. It wasn't bleeding. "Outside of this egg on my bean, I'm okay, I guess."

"You're lucky," Kevin said. "Matter of fact, we're both very lucky. This field is an old cow pasture, covered with holes and rocks. If we missed a hole, we'd have hit a rock. We were in for a rough ride no matter what."

They climbed out of the plane and were greeted by a loud hissing noise.

"Well," Kevin exclaimed, "a flat tire. I hope that's all this crate suffered. But I'd like to know what happened to the gas."

Jeff couldn't see that any visible damage had been done to the plane. It had taken a severe shaking, and that was all. Kevin stepped onto a wheel and took another look at the gas gauge. Jeff saw him strike the rod gently with the palm of his hand.

"Hey, what's this?" Kevin cried.

Jeff peered out.

"What's the matter, Kevin?"

Kevin unscrewed the cap and pulled out the gauge.

"No wonder!" he exclaimed. "This float gauge is homemade! It's about an inch too long!"

"You mean it shows there's gas inside the tank even if there isn't?" said Jeff.

"That's just exactly what happened," said Kevin. "This float was almost touching the bottom when we took off, showing enough gas to keep us flying for at least twenty minutes. As it was, we only had enough in there for about five! Phew!"

He screwed the cap back on.

"I'll fix that myself," he said. "But that's a lesson both of us should remember. Whenever you buy a second-hand plane, check every bit of it over thoroughly. You never know when some guy who thinks he's a mechanic has replaced a part with one he made himself, and didn't make it right."

They started trekking across the field toward the road.

"We'll go to that nearest farmhouse and put in a call to Barney Haddock," said Kevin.

The woman who answered the door was tall, thin-faced, and was wearing a blue lace-edged apron over her dress. From behind her came the sweet aroma of freshly baked apple pies.

"Hello, ma'am," Kevin said. "Our plane ran out of gas and we were forced to land in a field near by. Can we use your phone?"

The woman's expression was first one of surprise, then warmed with a friendly smile.

"Of course," she said. "Come on in."

Kevin made the call. Five minutes later, when he hung up, his expression was one of thorough disgust.

"Barney isn't there, and the joker who answered said that today is Sunday and mechanics don't work Sundays."

"What'll we do?" asked Jeff.

"I'll call Barney at his home," said Kevin.

He knew the Haddocks' number by heart because of frequent calls to Joan, so a moment later he was dialing again. This time he sported a satisfied smile when he hung up.

"That Barney is a real guy," he said. "He's coming over himself with a can of gas and a brand-new tire and tube."

Twenty minutes later Barney Haddock arrived in a station wagon. He had a ten-gallon container which, he said, wasn't full but had enough gas in it for him to fly the plane back to the airport. He also had a brand-new tire and tube.

Barney checked over the plane thoroughly. He was a man in his late forties, a veteran of World War II and the Korean conflict, and he knew planes from wing tip to wing tip and nose to tail. And of course he was Kevin's future father-in-law—which helped, thought Jeff.

Kevin removed the tire from the wheel and discovered a four-inch gash in its side. He put on the new tire and tube.

"Jeff, why don't you walk up to the other end of the field and see if it's any better there than it is here?" he said. "The land slopes up there, and there might not be as many holes."

"Okay," said Jeff.

He walked up to the far end of the pasture. As Kevin had figured, there weren't many holes there, owing, no doubt, to the fact that after a rain the water flowed down to the lower part of the field, making the ground wet and soggy and therefore gauged with hoofprints made by the cows.

Jeff returned and explained to Kevin what he had found.

"Good," said Kevin. "I'll taxi up there when we're done."

Fifteen minutes later Barney climbed off the plane, yanked an orange cloth out of his hip pocket and wiped his hands.

"I found a couple of sheered bolts on the engine mounting," he said, "and replaced them. Where are you going to take off?"

"Jeff said the ground isn't bad up at the other end of the field," Kevin replied. "If you're through we'll taxi up there and make our take-off."

"I'm through," said Barney. "But I'll walk over after you. If the ground is all right for a take-off, I can save you some space by holding on to your tail while you give her throttle."

"Fine," said Kevin. "Let's go, Jeff. By the way, Barney, bill me for the works."

"Who else?" Barney smiled.

Kevin started the motor, let it warm up a few moments, then taxied up to the other side of the field. The plane bumped and jogged over the hole-filled, stony ground.

They reached the upper side. Kevin looked out both windows, checked the ground, and agreed with Jeff that it was ready. Barney took hold of the tail, hung on grimly as Kevin pushed the throttle forward. The plane trembled with power, and then suddenly streaked ahead. The tail came up and the plane rolled roughly over the ground, gaining speed every second. Then the nose lifted and the roughness stopped. They were in the air.

What an experience this had been! thought Jeff, thinking back over the last frightening hour. Running out of gas . . . a forced landing on a rough field . . . a blowout . . . a bump on the head. And now, at last, a successful take-off—a happy finale to it all, instead of an unhappy disaster, which it might have been if luck had been against them.

Kevin circled the field, and both boys waved to Barney. Barney waved back.

"Right there's a great guy," Kevin said again, and directed the plane for home.

Only later did Jeff realize how calm Kevin had been during the entire ordeal. Kevin must have been a little frightened when he brought the dead-engined plane down on the rough pitted field. But he had handled the plane expertly. Jeff doubted if even Barney could have done better under the circumstances.

Jeff went to bed that night with a new respect for his older brother.

On Tuesday evening Kevin drove Jeff to school for their first league game—against South Hill High. Jeff didn't know whether he would start or not, but he wished Kevin would stay to watch the game. He got out of the car and the two brothers looked at each other for a long moment.

"Well, see you later," said Jeff. "Thanks for the lift."

"Jeff," Kevin said.

Jeff held the door he had been about to close.

"Yes?"

"I have a date with Joan," he said uneasily. "Otherwise I'd stay and watch the game."

Jeff forced a smile.

"Oh, that's all right, Kevin. See you."

Jeff closed the door.

Coach Stu Cochran started Eric Wilson and Sam Bullick at forward positions. Jeff warmed the bench. He had expected as much. The coach seemed always to do exactly what Jeff predicted.

Eric dumped in a set shot and a one-hand push-up in the first quarter. Jeff noticed that not a strand of hair on Eric's head had moved since the opening buzzer sounded. Yet he could not understand Coach

Cochran's strategy. South Hill was on top, 15–11, when the quarter ended.

Jeff started the second quarter, replacing Eric. But he was slow. He couldn't seem to get moving. His man was running all around him, taking passes, intercepting those meant for Jeff, and sinking more baskets than he'd been able to make against Eric.

There were two minutes left to go when Lee sank a basket for Carson and the buzzer sounded from the scorekeeper. Jeff was taken out.

"What's the matter, Jeff?" asked the coach. "You were running around out there as if you were carrying lead weights. Do you feel all right?"

"I feel okay," said Jeff.

"You're far from acting like it. I'm not going to ask what's troubling you, but whatever it is, try to shake it off. I want you to start the second half with Sam. With Gil gone, you're the next best player I have."

Jeff's mouth fell open. So he'd made the first string after all. He watched the coach. Stu Cochran's jaws were set squarely. His eyes were dead serious as they followed the game. Instantly Jeff took back every unfair thing he had ever thought about the coach. Who was he, anyway, to think he knew what went on in a busy coach's mind?

The second half started with Carson trailing, 19–28. The cheerleaders, after a rollicking cheer for the jayvees and a display of cartwheels and splits, ran off the floor, hands on hips, their short skirts flapping. The referee tossed the ball up between the two centers.

Lee's long arms waggled above his opponent's. His wrist snapped and the ball tipped to Jeff.

Jeff took it, pivoted, then dribbled away toward his basket. He crossed the center line, shot a pass to Eddie Russell who was running down the right side line, then broke fast behind the husky guard. Eddie flipped a two-handed chest pass to him. Jeff took it and went up high toward the basket. As he did so he shifted the ball to his right hand, gave it the extra push it needed, and saw it clear the rim.

Two points!

He raced back up court, the thoughts that had been plaguing him before entirely out of his mind now. He felt loose and tireless, much different from his mood during that miserable first half. He found that he missed Gil, though. Twice, when he had the ball, he looked around for Gil and, not seeing him, realized with fresh regret that Gil was no longer playing.

As the seconds passed, sensing Gil's absence was an incentive for Jeff. He played harder, knowing that it took every bit of skill he had, and probably more, to match Gil Baker's quick footwork, expert dribbling and passing on the floor. He found himself at the receiving end of the ball many times, which proved a point: he wasn't letting his man get in front of him; and he was moving, moving fast, darting here and there. Always on the alert. Taking the ball down to their basket, passing, feinting, dribbling in, sinking one after another through the hoop.

When the buzzer sounded the end of the third quarter, South Hill was still ahead, but the score was

closer. The electric scoreboard read: HOME–31, VIS-
ITORS–35.

Stu Cochran gave Lee Mattoon and Eddie Russell
a breather at the start of the fourth quarter. South
Hill sank two buckets in rapid succession. Then Jim
Barclay, the six-footer who substituted for Lee,
swooped up under the basket for a lay-up. Jeff pulled
a two-shot foul and made both shots. Carson picked
up four more points, and then both teams alternated
in sinking two baskets apiece.

With a two-minute margin Lee and Eddie came
back into the game. Filled with renewed energy and
ambition after a six minute rest, the tall center and
the husky guard helped spur their team on to a close
victory that brought cheers from the Carson fans
which practically made the building tremble.

Score: Carson–51, South Hill High–49.

Jeff had plenty of time to think while he showered
and dressed. He felt happy—happier than he had been
since the beginning of basketball season.

He knew now what he would tell his father. He had
made his decision. Flying lessons or not, he was not
going to drop out of basketball.

CHAPTER 8

THE ENTIRE jayvee and varsity teams congregated at Mike's Restaurant afterward. Jeff went with Lee and Eddie. The place filled quickly as fans also decided to cap the evening with a soda or ice cream.

Lee led the way to an empty stool. Jeff and Eddie followed and sat down beside him.

Just as Jeff made himself comfortable, a girl's voice called to him:

"Hi, Jeff."

He turned, and was surprised to see Joan Haddock seated at a table with her mother and father. The empty chair at the table was pushed far in, which indicated that it was not taken.

Where was Kevin? Jeff wondered.

They exchanged greetings.

"How did the games come out?" Joan asked.

"The jayvees won, fifty-one to forty-nine," Jeff said. "The varsity lost, sixty-eight to fifty-nine."

Joan smiled.

"Well, at least you fellows came through. How did you do?"

Jeff grinned.

"Eighteen points."

"Good! Well, I won't bother you any more, Jeff. Have your soda. And keep doing a good job."

"I'll try," said Jeff.

He unwrapped a straw and dipped it into the soda which a waitress had placed in front of him. He was beginning to think about Kevin when Mike, the owner of the restaurant, a smiling happy-go-lucky guy whose hair was always shorn in crewcut style, paused in front of them.

"Howdy, boys. So you won, huh, and the varsity lost?"

"That's right," said Lee.

"I thought that maybe losing Gil Baker might make a big difference with you guys."

"We miss him, all right," said Lee. "Gil's a good man."

"Just play hard and put all you got into it," Mike said with the authority of an old-timer, although he was only about twenty-eight himself, an age at which a lot of ballplayers were still in their prime. "That's all you have to do. Play like you mean it. Get a lot of sleep. Maybe you might even beat the varsity."

"Hey, cut that out," said one of the varsity players sitting a little farther down the counter. "What do you want to do, break down our confidence?"

Mike laughed.

"You guys need more than confidence. I'll have to stop in some time and show you how a pro can play."

The boys laughed.

Mike wiped his hands with a white cloth as he walked over to take their orders. Jeff sipped his soda and thought of Kevin. Kevin had said he had a date with Joan, but Joan was here with her mother and father. If he hadn't wanted to see the game, why didn't he say so?

Jeff was sure, too, that Kevin hadn't seen Joan at all that night. Joan would surely have mentioned it, if he had.

Jeff emptied the glass. A few minutes later Lee and Eddie were ready to leave with him. When he arrived home he found that his mother and dad had gone to bed. A light in the living room was left burning for him.

He stepped quietly across the carpeted floor and was about to turn off the light when he remembered Kevin. Was he home? Or had he actually gone out? He wouldn't be seeing another girl, Jeff was sure of that. Where could he have gone and what could he have done that was so important he had to lie?

"Jeff, is that you?" his mother called from the bedroom.

"Yes, Mom," said Jeff softly.

"Don't turn out the light or lock the door," she said. "Kevin hasn't come home yet."

"Okay, Mom."

His heart pounded. He went to his room, got undressed. He told himself it wasn't his business what Kevin did. Yet Kevin had lied to him. If he wasn't with Joan, then where was he? Why had he lied?

It was only minutes later when Jeff heard the outside door open and close. He heard Kevin go to his room, and then all was silent.

At breakfast Kevin appeared his usual self, said nothing of his activity the night before. He was interested in how Carson had made out in both the jayvee and varsity games, and in how many points Jeff had scored.

Jeff told him, but tried hard to avoid Kevin's eyes. Whether Kevin noticed or not, he made no issue of it. Jeff wished he had. Kevin's lie bothered him, and he was willing to express himself if Kevin brought the matter up.

Mr. Dooley said nothing about the game, but that wasn't unusual. Jeff wondered, though, how his father would react when he told him that he wasn't dropping out of basketball.

Mr. Gregory met Jeff in the school corridor, and, of all things, he smiled.

"Good morning, Jeff. How are you?"

"I'm fine. How are you?"

Mr. Gregory chuckled.

"I understand that in spite of Gil's dropping out of basketball you boys won the jayvee game last night."

"That's right," said Jeff.

"That's good." The science teacher rubbed his forefinger and thumb together thoughtfully. "Gil received a failing mark the other day in the test. I was sorry for him. I had a feeling he wouldn't pass."

Jeff moistened his lips.

"What did I get?"

"You did unusually well. You surprised me." He paused, nodded to several students who were passing by, and showed his best early morning smile. It seemed to Jeff that he was deliberately delaying his answer in order to provoke him.

Finally Mr. Gregory turned back to Jeff.

"You got an eighty-four," he said. "It's a pretty good mark, but you should have done even better."

Jeff felt only relief. The mark was better than he had expected.

"We're having another test some time this week," Mr. Gregory said. "You understand that if your average is below seventy in any one of your subjects, you're prohibited from playing basketball."

"Yes. I understand," Jeff said.

Mr. Gregory lifted a hand in a wave, and grinned mildly.

"I'll be seeing you, Jeff," he said. He turned and walked to his home room across the hall.

Jeff eyed his narrow back for a few seconds, then closed his lips tightly and headed for his locker to gather up his books.

There was practice after school. Jeff concentrated on the one-hand pivot shot. He had read in a magazine that this is a difficult shot but a good one once it is mastered. The play starts with a pass to a man stationed with his back to the basket. The man catches the pass with both hands. He fakes his guard with his body, or feints with his hand to draw him off. Then he steps with his left foot at an angle toward the basket. He shifts the ball to his right hand and leaps high for the basket, snapping the ball up and in with his wrist.

The first and second stringers scrimmaged, and Jeff, playing with the first team, tried the pivot play whenever possible and found himself improving. Eric Wilson guarded him. For a while Jeff fooled Eric consistently with his body fake or hand feint until Eric got rough and committed a couple of fouls. Eric didn't seem to mind mussing up his hair now, perhaps because there was no crowd watching.

After twenty minutes, Coach Cochran shifted some of the players around, putting Bill Godell and Eric in as forwards on the first team, Jeff and Red Mason, a slender boy with glasses, on the second team.

Jeff played opposite Bruce, who turned out to be a rugged guard, faster on his feet than he looked. Twice Jeff tried the pivot shot on Bruce, and was successful both times.

"Say! Nice shooting!" cried Bruce. "But I'll stop you the next time!"

Jeff laughed. That was what he wanted, a good guard to try to stop him. That was the best type of practice.

The next time he tried the pivot shot, taking the pass from Red Mason, Bruce came in too close and, in trying to knock the ball out of Jeff's hands, struck Jeff's arm. Stu Cochran called a foul, and Jeff grinned at Bruce.

"You're doing all right, Jeff," said Bruce, smiling back.

Jeff appreciated the compliment. He made the shot.

Bruce took the ball out and passed to Lee. Lee fired a one-hand pass down the length of the court to Eddie Russell. Eddie caught it, dribbled in, and pushed in a one-hand lay-up without any trouble.

"Who's his man?" shouted Jeff. "Keep him covered!"

He saw Mason rush to cover Eddie on the next play, but the boy was not very effective against Eddie, whose clever footwork made up for his weakness in shooting baskets. Eddie pulled Mason aside with a feint, drove in and planted another neat lay-up that tapped lightly against the backboard and fluttered through the net.

Jeff saw that Eddie was having the time of his life. He dumped in two more shots in less than thirty seconds. The coach called time, and put Red against Bruce and Eric against Eddie. Bruce tried to repeat Eddie's performance, but his aim was off. He sank in two long set shots, however, which drew one measure of a chorus from him and a two-second exhibition of tap dancing.

"Okay. Cut the clowning," snapped the coach. But he was amused, as Jeff could see by the half smile on his lips.

They were at it for another half hour, then the coach called it quits for the day.

"Practice tomorrow afternoon," he said, "then the game with Westfield Central on Friday at Westfield. Okay. The showers."

That evening after dinner Jeff sat in the family living room reading the sports page of the local newspaper. His father lounged on the davenport opposite watching the news on TV. Jeff had just finished an article on the Celtics' close game with St. Louis when his father's voice broke in on his thoughts:

"Jeff."

Jeff lowered the paper, and looked over at his father. His heart pounded.

"Yes, Dad?"

"How's basketball going?"

It was the first time in many days that his father had mentioned basketball.

"Okay, Dad."

"Are you going to continue playing?"

Jeff took a deep breath.

"Yes, Dad," he said. "I want very much to continue playing."

Mr. Dooley turned his attention back to the TV set. He didn't say a word.

CHAPTER 9

ONLY A FEW Westfield fans studded the Westfield High gym at game time. A moment before the game started, Westfield's junior varsity cheerleaders, trim and pert in black and white uniforms, gave a locomotive yell. Then the Carson jayvees' cheerleaders hopped out on the floor, formed the letter C, and shouted:

> "Jeff Dooley, he's our man!
> If he can't do it, Bullick can!
> Sam Bullick, he's our man!
> If he can't do it, Mattoon can!
> Lee Mattoon, he's our man!
> If he can't do it, Russell can!
> Eddie Russell, he's our man!
> If he can't do it, Parker can!
> Bruce Parker, he's our man!
> If he can't do it, Cochran can!
> Coach Cochran, he's our man!
> If he can't do it, *Nobody* can!"

The cheer ended with a tremendous roar from the Carson side of the court. The girls skipped off the floor, and the teams took over.

The Westfield center was an inch taller than Lee Mattoon, but much thinner. The two boys crouched. There was that breathless moment that always prevails just before the referee tosses the ball into the air. Jeff, standing with his knees slightly bent, ready to move the instant the ball was tapped, breathed with the nervous tension that took hold of him the first few moments before a game started. But there was something more on his mind, the fear that he had let his father down.

The Westfield center out-jumped Lee, tapping the ball with the tips of his long fingers directly at a husky-shouldered blond boy. The blond dribbled away, but Eddie, sticking close, forced him to pass. Jeff's man took the ball and dribbled hard down the side of the court, Jeff racing along behind him. He stopped abruptly, pivoted, and flung an overhand pass between Jeff's raised, outstretched arms. Another Westfield man took the ball, drove in for lay-up, and made it.

Jeff shook his head. He could have prevented that basket if he had been alert when that pass was made.

Carson took the ball out of bounds, marched it down the court. Jeff received it in the three-second lane and passed to Bruce. Bruce feinted a throw for the basket, shot quickly to Lee. Just then the whistle shrilled.

"Three seconds!" the referee shouted.

Jeff looked at the official. The referee was pointing at him!

"Come on! Let's go, Jeff!" Sam Bullick yelled.

Jeff lowered his head in disgust. He wasn't alert. He wasn't thinking. Normally he would never have stood there three seconds.

Westfield passed the ball to the other end of the court. Jeff ashamed of his poor playing so far, plunged in to break the Westfield play. Shoulders brushed shoulders as half a dozen players in black and white and black and orange uniforms fought for possession of the ball. A pair of hands clamped on it, picked the ball off the floor.

Jeff slapped at the ball. It bounced away. Westfield retrieved it.

"You crazy goon!" Bruce Parker shouted at him. "You knocked it out of my hands!"

Jeff flushed.

"I'm sorry, Bruce. I thought—"

"Never mind," said Bruce. "Forget it. Let's get it back."

The ball was already on Westfield's side of the court. Westfield moved in fast. A quick break, a left knee rising off the floor, the ball arching toward the backboard—then a basket.

The buzzer sounded from the bench. Eric came in, tapped Jeff on the shoulder.

"The bench, bub. Who's your man?"

Jeff, breathing tiredly, glared at him.

"Number 4," he said, and ran off the court, his head bowed.

He sat in the vacant space Eric had left for him.

"Nice game," said Red Mason.

Yeah, Jeff thought. Nice game, all right. Kid, anybody could play a lousy game out there for four full quarters and you'd still say, "Nice game."

The first period ended.

Carson was trailing, 9–4.

Carson fought back in the second quarter, led by Lee Mattoon who played brilliantly this period. He dumped in four baskets, all lay-ups, and the tall West-field center was helpless against him. Eric sank another, and made good on a foul shot. Westfield had to be satisfied with four points, which made the score at the end of the half Carson–15, Westfield–13.

"Something was bothering you out there," Lee said to Jeff as the two boys sat together on the bench in the locker room. "What's the matter?"

Jeff shook his head.

"Nothing. Guess I just couldn't get started."

"Boy, when you knocked that ball out of my hands, I thought you were nuts," Bruce said. "Didn't you see that I had it?"

"That's a smart question," said Sam Bullick, drying his face with a towel. "Would he have knocked the ball out of your hands if he saw that you had it?"

"Let's cut the talk," Coach Cochran said. "Anybody could have done what Jeff did. We have a two-point lead. That's not much. Let's keep fighting and take this one home in our pockets. The same five men who started the first quarter will start the second half."

Jeff glanced at the coach. Stu Cochran gazed at him briefly, then lifted the sleeve of his suit coat and looked at his watch.

Jeff was surprised to be in the starting line-up for

the second half. He hadn't done anything in the first half to deserve it.

Lee started where he had left off in the first half, scoring twice in succession. Then Westfield started in like a new team. They sank four buckets and drew three foul shots, scoring one. One of the foul shots was chalked against Jeff. He himself tried four set shots, but each time the ball barely touched the rim of the basket. He was off, and off bad. With five seconds left in the third period, he caught a pass from Lee and laid one up against the backboard that whistled through the net, and he hoped now that the spell had broken.

Eric started the last quarter, and Jeff didn't go in again. He was glad, for he certainly was a hindrance to the team today, rather than an asset. Nevertheless, as Coach Cochran had hoped, the jayvees won the game, 40–37.

Jeff remained quiet on the ride home in the bus. He sat next to the window, with Lee. Lee chattered away with Bruce and Eddie practically all the way back to Carson. If anyone noticed Jeff's silence, no one let on.

He couldn't go on like this very long, he thought. A sourpuss was as noticeable as a purple cow, and he had better act sensible about what was bothering him before the kids started hurling embarrassing questions at him.

Carson beat Brighton, 38–25. Jeff played all but a few minutes of the game, ranking second in points only to Lee Mattoon. Lee had scored seventeen, Jeff fifteen. Already word was going around that Jeff was another Gil Baker. He did that pivot shot, receiving a ball with his back to the basket, just as Gil used to do it. But after all, Jeff thought, how else could you perform the shot?

The next game was with Lincoln, the team Carson had played in a practice tilt the week before the league started. Lincoln had won that game and Carson was determined to take this one.

The game went into a two-minute overtime period as the fourth quarter ended at a deadlock, 47–47. Lee scored, and then fouled out with five fouls against him. Jim Barclay replaced him.

Lincoln made the first foul shot, missed the second. The red lights on the electric time clock showed the seconds skipping by. Carson was still ahead, 49–48.

Thirty seconds to go . . . twenty-five . . . twenty . . .

A Lincoln man had the ball and bounce-passed it across the floor. Jeff spotted the play and charged at the tall player who had caught the pass. The player was running in under the basket, ready to make a shot. Jeff leaped up beside him and struck his hand.

Shrieeeeeek!

The referee held up eight fingers, then pointed at Jeff. Jeff lifted his arm.

"Two shots," said the referee.

The crowd's response was deafening. The Carson cheerleaders jumped out on the floor and gave a cheer for Jeff.

"One! Two! Three! Four!
Who are we for!

Dooley! Dooley!
Ray!"

The Lincoln cheerleaders, not to be outdone, came onto the floor next.

"Do what the Navy does!
Sink it!"

Then the big gym became silent. The Lincoln player took the ball in both hands, measured the basket with his eyes, dipped his knees and shot, pushing the ball from his chest.

It went in!

Screams tore from the throats of fans on both sides. The bleachers, which had been almost empty when the game started, were now packed like shelves in a supermarket.

Suddenly there was silence again as the referee gave a short blast on his whistle and held up one finger. He handed the ball to the Lincoln player for the second shot. The boy took a deep breath, let it out, aimed at the basket. He shot exactly as he had before. It went in.

A few seconds later the final buzzer blew. Lincoln was the winner, 50–49.

A hand gripped Jeff's. Jeff looked up to see the smiling face of the boy he had purposely charged.

"Nice game," the boy said. "You played it right, but I was lucky."

Jeff grinned.

"Thanks. You were sure to make it the other way. I had to take the chance."

"I know," said the Lincoln player. "You did all right. See you next time." He ran off to join his teammates.

Jeff headed for the locker room. *You did all right.* The words kept ringing in his mind. He wondered whether he had.

CHAPTER 10

THE CARSON JAYVEES nosed out a victory over Washington, 28–25, the last game before Christmas vacation. Coach Cochran reminded the boys that there was practice every morning Monday through Saturday from nine-thirty to twelve. The only exceptions were Christmas Day and New Year's.

Snow flurries filled the air Saturday morning. Jeff felt sure he would not have a flying lesson today. He telephoned to check. Joan Haddock answered. After talking with Jim Tucker, she said that Jim thought they'd better wait for a decent day.

"I'm having Christmas vacation," said Jeff. "I can come over any afternoon when it's nice."

"Okay, Jeff. I'll tell Jim. He can call you when he thinks the weather's suitable."

On Sunday morning Jeff and Kevin drove to the middle of town and bought a Christmas tree. Both boys cleared a corner of the living room, put up the tree, and decorated it. It had been a yearly ritual ever since Jeff was old enough to go to school. The many different colored lights were turned on, and packages piled underneath. From his savings, which he had accumulated from a weekly allowance and an occasional dollar or two from Kevin, Jeff had bought gifts for his family.

A few days before Christmas, snow fell and left a white blanket over the city. For two days a severe wind howled through the streets, which canceled any possibility of flying lessons for that week, at least. Jeff had little desire to fly, anyway. He realized that while he was in the plane, flying over the city and the hills surrounding it, he was filled with the enjoyment of flying. But when he was away from it, he did not yearn to go up again right away. It wasn't like basketball, which haunted him almost every minute of the day when he wasn't preoccupied with something else.

Kevin's mysterious Tuesday night trips bothered Jeff. Twice since that first Tuesday night, Kevin had done the same thing. He hadn't said where he was going the last two times, except "out."

"I don't know where he goes or what he does," his mother said to Jeff when he asked her about it. "After all, if it's something he doesn't want us to know, it's his business. Maybe it has something to do with his job. His work is very much like your father's, you know. Whatever they do is entirely secret. They could be heavily penalized for talking about their work."

The explanation sounded reasonable. Jeff wondered why he hadn't thought of it before. Yet he wasn't completely satisfied. Kevin would have said as much if it was something to do with his work. He certainly wouldn't have lied about having a date with Joan.

Jeff had always felt sure he knew his brother Kevin

almost as well as he knew himself. Now, he wasn't so sure.

On Christmas Eve the Dooleys opened their Christmas packages. Later Kevin went to Joan's, with a gift from himself and one from the family.

The Haddocks came over for dinner on Christmas Day. After the long hearty dinner, the menfolk congregated in the living room to talk and watch television, while the ladies washed the dishes.

At first Barney Haddock and Mr. Dooley discussed local politics and the sewage disposal plan the city was going to start work on in the spring. Jeff was bored listening. He wanted to go out and visit some of his own friends, but felt that it wouldn't be proper to leave—not with company there.

Suddenly Barney turned to Jeff.

"How're the jayvees doing, Jeff?"

Jeff was surprised at the question. He didn't know Barney Haddock well, didn't know how interested he was in sports, other than flying.

"All right," Jeff said.

"I must go down and see you play some time. Joan tells me you're pretty good."

Jeff blushed.

"Oh—fair," he said.

He glanced at his father. Mr. Dooley had turned his attention to TV. His jaw was set, his mouth tightly closed.

"When's your next game?" Barney Haddock asked.

"First Tuesday after New Year's," replied Jeff. "We're playing South Hill High. Over there."

"I'll try to make the next home game," said Barney. He shook his head, and a smile played across his lips. "Boy, every time I talk sports I get to thinking about my age. It doesn't seem possible that I've been out of the game twenty years."

Jeff raised his eyebrows.

"Don't tell me you used to play basketball, Mr. Haddock!"

Barney Haddock chuckled.

"I played in high school and then on a town team. Played a good many years, too. Even after I was married and Joan was born. Your dad might remember that. But maybe he doesn't." He looked at Jeff's father. "That must have been about the time you went to Western Tech, wasn't it, Rob? And from there to—what university was it again?"

"M.I.T.," Kevin answered for his father. "Massachusetts Institute of Technology."

"Oh, yes. That's right." Barney Haddock chuckled again. "Your dad went on to better things while I stuck around playing basketball and baseball, and working at any job I could find until I joined the Air Corps. Ever since then I've been in the flying business."

Jeff nodded and smiled. But he ached inwardly. If only his dad shared Barney's obvious enthusiasm for sports. Mr. Dooley hadn't said a word during Jeff's and Barney's exchange. What exactly can he have against the game, anyway? Jeff wondered. Why do I have to be different from him? *The last thing I ever want to do is hurt my dad.*

Barney Haddock must have noticed Mr. Dooley's

silence for he turned to Jeff's father and asked him how things were going at Dunnigan.

The next morning, Jeff left for basketball practice with a heavy heart. Was he selfish to be acting against his father's wishes? Was he wrong in thinking that it was all right to play basketball so long as his marks were satisfactory? After all, that was what his father was mainly after, wasn't it? To keep his marks up?

Jeff pondered. It looked as though his father didn't want him to play basketball, period—no matter what his marks were.

I don't know what to think, Jeff thought. I just don't know what to do.

Vacation finally came to an end, and Jeff went back to school.

"I'm not coming home after school, Mom," Jeff told his mother before leaving the house Tuesday morning. "We're going to South Hill."

"I hope the weather clears up a little," Mrs. Dooley said. "The radio said it's fifteen degrees and there'll be snow before nightfall."

Jeff grinned.

"Don't worry, Mom. A little snow never hurt anybody."

"What time can we expect you home?"

"We'll be staying for the varsity game, too, so it won't be before eleven or eleven-thirty."

"Okay. Just so I don't worry my silly head off," she said, smiling.

It snowed on and off during the day.

At noontime some of the jayvee players, including Jeff, sat in the gym bleachers watching a foul-shooting tournament among the fifth, sixth, and seventh graders.

"I hope tonight's game won't be canceled on account of the weather," said Bruce. "I hate postponed games."

"Me, too," said Lee.

The game wasn't postponed, although by the time the buses left there were two or three inches of snow on the ground.

Eric Wilson, sitting with Bruce, acted a little cocky.

"Let's swamp 'em tonight," he said. "We had to come up from behind the last time to beat 'em. Let's get a head start this time."

"Don't get too overconfident, my fair-haired friend," said Bruce. "They might swamp *us*."

"Dah!" said Eric. Eric had the right idea, of course, but it wasn't that easy. The first quarter was almost a repetition of their first game. South Hill picked up a ten-point lead, and in the second period widened it by sixteen points. Jeff's pivot shot and lay-ups weren't working regularly, and neither were Lee's. Sam Bullick was dropping in a set shot now and then, and Bruce and Eddie were doing their share. But it wasn't enough.

Coach Cochran started Eric in place of Jeff in the second half, and alternated the other players during the rest of the game. But South Hill had the upper hand from the beginning, and kept it. When the final buzzer sounded, the score was South Hill–52, Carson–28.

Later, after the varsity game, which Carson won 64–59, the buses took off, carrying cheerleaders and a load of boys, some happy, some solemn.

"I told you, didn't I?" Bruce said to Eric. "Maybe you should have kept your trap shut."

"I guess so," admitted Eric humbly.

Jeff could see that Eric felt as bad about losing the game as anyone. He looked at the smaller boy thoughtfully and realized how his feelings toward Eric had changed. Maybe his previous judgment of his teammate had been mistaken. After all, what had Eric done that was so bad, anyway?

The bus rumbled on through the night, the two windshield wipers swishing rhythmically back and forth, wiping off the snow that was falling thick and hard against the windshields. The spectators' bus ahead was long out of sight.

In the distance Jeff heard a faint wail. He soon distinguished it as the blast of a train. He wiped the mist off the window beside him and looked out. What a lousy night, he thought. He wished he was home in bed.

The blast sounded again and again. Each time it was closer. Jeff saw the light—a big yellow eye—shooting a cone-shaped ray through the snowy darkness. The crossing couldn't be far away.

SHRIEEEEEEEK!

The roaring blast seemed to come from just outside the bus now.

Then the bus jerked, knocking Jeff back against the seat, throwing Lee against him. Jeff had his eyes on

Mr. Kerns, the bus driver, and sudden fright filled them.

He saw Mr. Kerns turn the wheel. In the rear-view mirror the bus driver's face was stricken with panic, his eyes wide. Jeff had never seen a look like that before. He clenched the top of the seat in front of him and hung on tightly.

The kids had been talking all the time. Some of the cheerleaders were singing. No one seemed to notice what was happening until the last minute.

Just then the front end of the bus tilted downward as the wheels went off the road. The vehicle rocked violently. Jeff bounced against Lee, almost knocking him to the floor.

In the back seat the girls screamed.

CHAPTER 11

THE BUS rocked like a boat struck by a series of heavy waves. Springs and joints squealed. Jeff hung on desperately. He tried to look ahead through the front windshield, but he couldn't see anything distinctly, only the swirling snow falling outside.

And then the bus shuddered to a stop. The screams ended. For a moment no one moved.

Mr. Kerns turned around in his seat. His face was pasty white, his eyes wide.

"Everybody all right?" he said.

"I'm okay," Jeff said. "How about you, Lee?"

"I'm okay, too," said Lee.

"The coach is hurt!" somebody in front said.

"Mary Jane's hurt her shoulder," somebody else said.

Jeff heard sobs behind him. He turned and saw a blonde cheerleader resting her face against the shoulder of the girl beside her. She was crying.

"What happened, Jim?" somebody yelled.

The bus driver rose from his seat and faced the students. He took out a handkerchief and mopped his brow.

"The brakes weren't taking hold," he said shakily. "They must have gotten wet. The only thing I could do was turn off the road. I—I hope nobody's seriously hurt."

"Coach Cochran is," the same voice that had spoken before said. Jeff recognized Mike Catoddi's voice. Mike was a senior and a forward on the varsity.

Mike got up and faced Mr. Kerns.

"That farmhouse we passed wasn't too far back, was it, Jim?"

"About a quarter of a mile," the bus driver said.

"Better call the sheriff, and also Mr. Gallagher," Jeff heard Cochran say in a hoarse voice. "Have him send over another bus. Think you can back this bus out, Jim?"

Jim Kerns shook his head.

"Not a chance. Nothing but a wrecker, or a tractor, could pull us out."

"Those farmers back up the road should have at least one tractor," the coach said. "Ask them if they'd try it. We'll pay for it."

"Okay," said Jim Kerns. "Come on, Mike."

Two state trooper cars arrived fifteen minutes later. Behind them was an ambulance. They got there just moments before the farmer came with his John Deere tractor.

A trooper stepped into the lighted bus. Behind him came a bespectacled, broad-shouldered man.

"Anybody hurt?" the trooper said.

"Coach Cochran," someone in front said.

"And Mary Jane back here."

"Okay. This is Dr. Neilson. He'll check you over."

The doctor spent several minutes examining the basketball coach. The students sat quietly. Jeff was aware of silent tense faces and anxious eyes.

Finally the doctor stood up.

"The coach has suffered some external lacerations that I can take care of now," he said. "But he's also injured internally. He'd better be taken to the hospital."

Lee turned and looked at Jeff.

"Did you hear that?"

Jeff just shook his head for an answer.

Mary Jane also seriously hurt, was examined next.

"She'd better be taken, too," said the doctor.

Two other girls were also removed from the bus and placed in the ambulance with the coach and Mary Jane. They needed treatment for shock. Everyone else was asked to leave the bus. The farmer, a raw-boned young man dressed in heavy winter clothing, secured a chain to the back end of the bus and to the rear of his tractor. Jim Kerns got behind the wheel of the bus and started the motor. With the tractor pulling, and the bus aiding under its own power, the big vehicle soon lumbered out of the ditch.

Jim steered it to the right side of the road. Cars had accumulated in both directions.

"Okay. Everybody back inside the bus," snapped one of the troopers.

The students piled back in. The troopers waved the cars on, first those from one direction, then those from the other.

Jeff, sitting again with Lee, shivered.

"I hope that other bus gets here quick," he said. "It's real cold in here."

"I wonder what we're going to do with this bus?" said Lee.

It was twenty-five minutes before the other bus arrived. It turned around at the farmhouse, then drove up behind Jim Kerns' bus. The students crowded in. Then the new bus started off and Jim Kerns followed in his bus. They drove all the way to the bus garage, where they left Mr. Kerns and were driven to school.

Jeff's mother and father got out of bed when Jeff arrived home.

"Jeff! Where have you been?" Mrs. Dooley's eyes were wide with anxiety. "It's almost two o'clock."

"We had a little trouble," said Jeff. "Not much. Mr. Kerns had to drive the bus into a ditch. The brakes didn't hold."

"Ditch?" His father's eyes widened, too. "Why into a ditch? What happened?"

Jeff felt tired.

"A train was coming. We couldn't run into it, could we? So we ran off into a ditch. That was the only thing to do, wasn't it?"

He realized he was annoyed. He should have thought twice before bursting out like that to his father. He started past his parents toward his room.

His father grabbed his arm.

"This is the last time," he said sternly. His eyes narrowed angrily. "Your mother and I were worrying about you every minute. No more basketball for you."

Jeff was stunned by his father's commanding words. He went to his room and closed the door behind him. His father just didn't understand! Something like that could happen any time, even with a car. He *must* know that.

Well, thought Jeff, he's finally got his way. He never wanted me to play basketball, and that was the perfect excuse to make me quit.

The next day at school everyone was talking about the bus incident. Word had been received from the hospital that the three girls were coming home today, but the coach had to stay for another few days.

Jeff was anxious about Coach Cochran. So were all his teammates and the cheerleaders and many others. The coach was a popular figure.

"I hope he'll be back by the next time we play," Eddie Russell said. "We're lost without him."

"Coach Wilkins'll take over," said Lee. Wilkins was the varsity coach.

Jeff kept silent. It wasn't till noon that he could bring himself to tell Lee Mattoon what his father had said that morning.

Lee was amazed.

"What? What's the matter with your dad? Is he nuts?"

Jeff shrugged.

"He's against basketball and every other sport except flying. He never wanted me to play in the first place. Do me a favor, Lee," Jeff added. "Please don't mention this to anybody. You're the only one I've ever told."

"Sure, Jeff," said Lee. "You can trust me. Then you won't be at our practice tonight?"

"No."

Lee shook his head. "We might as well fold up. Gil's quit, and now you—the two best players on the team."

"Oh, cut it out," said Jeff. "I was far from the best."

"You were coming along fast, though. Your eye was getting better all the time. You've really been hitting, Jeff."

"Well, I was improving, I guess," admitted Jeff.

He had to tell the other members of the team that he wouldn't be at practice today. He couldn't avoid that. Or tomorrow they'd hound him like a pack of dogs about why he hadn't shown up. Might as well let them know now.

Before lunch hour was over, Jeff had told the rest of his teammates of his intention to quit. They demanded an explanation, but his only reply was a shrug, and the excuse, "I just have to. Don't keep asking me why. I just have to, that's all. That's it. Period."

When Kevin arrived home from work that evening he was surprised to see Jeff.

"What? No practice today?"

"I'm done," Jeff said.

"Done? What do you mean?"

"After our bus accident last night, Dad told me that was it. I can't play basketball any more."

"Oh. I see."

Kevin walked away. Jeff's gaze followed Kevin's broad back. He wondered if Kevin, too, was really against basketball like their father. It was difficult to tell what Kevin thought, for he seldom spoke about the game. But then, Kevin was keeping counsel about something else, too—his regular Tuesday night outings.

Mary Jane, and the two girls who had suffered from shock, returned to school two days later. Coach Cochran was still out. That night the boys on the jayvee team decided to pay him a visit.

"He's home," Lee said. "Maybe you should tell him, Jeff."

"You mean about me quitting?"

Lee nodded.

"Maybe I should," agreed Jeff.

Jeff was nervous as he and the boys walked the eight blocks to Coach Cochran's house that night. Mrs. Cochran met them at the door with a gracious smile and invited them all in. The coach was resting in a chair.

"Boy! Is that soft!" joked Lee.

The coach laughed. "Too soft," he said. "I'm getting lazy."

"How long do you have to be here?" someone asked.

"The doc said he'd check me again next week, and probably a week after that it'll be okay for me to get back to work."

The talk drifted to other subjects and Jeff noticed Lee glance at him meaningfully. He summoned all his courage. If the fellows hadn't known of his intentions he would never do this in front of them.

"Coach," he said, and moistened his dry lips.

"Yes, Jeff?"

"I thought I'd better tell you," Jeff said nervously. "I—well, I've quit basketball."

The coach was shocked.

"What? What's the trouble? Are your marks down? They were fine the last time I heard."

"It isn't my marks. But that's what it might turn out to be. I mean I—" Jeff swallowed. His heart pounded. "I'll tell you some other time. Is that all right, Mr. Cochran?"

"Okay. We'll leave it that way, Jeff. But, my goodness, Gil Baker before, and now you! Who will it be next?"

Lee laughed.

"The rest of us are going to stick it out, coach," he said.

"I hope so!" said Coach Cochran. "Or I'll have to start looking for another job!"

Jeff missed three games. And then, on Friday, the day of the game with Westfield, Jeff heard his name over the public address system as he sat in the study hall.

"Jeffrey Dooley, please report to my office. This is Mr. Gallagher."

Jeff stared at the round speaker on the wall as if it were alive. He felt all eyes turn to him, felt them on him as he rose and walked out. Now what? he thought.

Mr. Gallagher greeted him with a smile, which quickly relieved some of his anxiety.

"Hi, Jeff. Sit down."

"Thank you," said Jeff.

The principal turned his tall slender form around on

the swivel chair, crossed his arms, and faced Jeff.

"I hear you've quit the jayvee basketball team," he said. "Do you mind telling me your reason?"

Jeff pursed his lips. Was *this* why Mr. Gallagher wanted to see him?

"Well—it's hard to tell, sir."

"I've checked your marks. I know it isn't that. Is it something personal? Something you don't want me to know?"

Jeff bit his lip.

"Well, sir—I just don't know how to say it."

"Do you like basketball, Jeff?"

"I love it."

"I thought so. Then is it something at home? I noticed this happened the day after Mr. Kerns' bus went off the road. That have something to do with your quitting?"

Jeff was amazed at Mr. Gallagher's insight.

"Partly," he said.

"Partly?" The principal frowned. "What do you mean by 'partly,' Jeff?"

Jeff looked down at his hands. They were trembling.

"It's my dad, Mr. Gallagher. He's never wanted me to play basketball or any other sport. When that accident happened he cracked down. When I came into the house he and my mother were still awake. I guess they were pretty worried."

"What did he say, Jeff?"

"He said, 'This is the last time. No more basketball for you.' "

"So that's it," said Mr. Gallagher thoughtfully.

"Yes, sir."

Mr. Gallagher tapped a pencil against his desk top.

"All right, Jeff. You may go back to your room now. Thanks for coming down."

Jeff walked out of the office. He wondered if he had done the right thing in telling Mr. Gallagher the truth.

When Mr. Dooley got home from the laboratory that evening, he greeted each member of his family as always. But today Jeff detected something different in his father's greeting. He seemed quieter than usual. There seemed to be something on his mind. But it wasn't until they sat down to supper that he brought out the reason for his quietness.

"Jeff," he said, "whatever I said to you that night you came home late from the basketball game—forget it."

Jeff started.

"What do you mean, Dad?"

"Go back to your basketball!" his father exploded. Mr. Dooley had spoken loudly, but he wasn't angry. In a quieter voice, he went on: "It seems that I'm an old carpetbagger, lacking in respect for one of the greatest games in history, a game which draws a larger audience than any other; a game that not only builds muscles but brains, too. That's something somebody neglected to tell me thirty years ago."

Jeff hardly knew what to think. No one but Mr. Gallagher, who had known Jeff's father for years, could have dared to say such things to Mr. Dooley and get away with it.

"So that's it," concluded Mr. Dooley. "I forgot to mention that you seem to be sort of a hero down there. One good player has already quit the team. If you quit, the jayvees might as well wrap themselves up and fade away. I would never want to be the cause of such a devastating catastrophe."

Jeff saw his mother and Kevin smile across the table. Kevin winked.

Jeff tried hard to control his excitement.

"Thanks, Dad," he said. "But—"

"But what?" said his father.

"I won't play unless you, Mom, and Kevin come to watch our next home game."

Mr. Dooley made a face.

"No, sir! Count me out! I'm not going to watch any basketball game!"

"Then I won't play," said Jeff.

"You're a fool!" roared his father.

"Okay. I'm a fool."

Mrs. Dooley smiled at her son.

"Don't worry," she said confidently. "He'll go. So will I, and so will Kevin."

CHAPTER **12**

THE WASHINGTON game was to be played away. Kevin drove Jeff to the school, where they arrived just as the buses were about to leave.

"Hey! Look who's here! It's Jeff Dooley!"

"Jeff! Hey! Wow, man! Hooray!"

Jeff heard the yells as he hopped out of Kevin's car.

"Play hard, and good luck!" Kevin shouted to him as Jeff closed the car door and waved.

He climbed into the bus and was greeted with loud applause. Then the girls yelled.

"One! Two! Three! Four!
Who are we for!
J-E-F-F! Jeff! Hooray!"

"Hi, Jeff!" cried Lee Mattoon, smiling from ear to ear.

"Hi, Lee!"

"Hi, Jeffrey!"

"Hiya, ol' pal!"

"Glad to see ya, kid! You just made it!"

Jeff's heart sang as if it were filled with bells. He was back on the squad! Good ol' Mr. Gallagher. Jeff wished he could have tapped the telephone conversation between Mr. Gallagher and his father, and then seen his father's face. Boy!

The Washington jayvees hopped around the court with cocky jauntiness during the pre-game warm-up. They had lost the first game against Carson and were looking for a victory.

Coach Wilkins used the same starting line-up in the jayvee game that had played against South Hill High: Jeff and Sam at the forward positions, Lee at center, Bruce and Eddie at guard.

Washington was iron hot from the moment the buzzer sounded, seizing the ball and moving it down toward their basket as if it were magnetized to them. In fifteen seconds they had a basket. Carson took out the ball. Seconds later a Washington man intercepted and the ball again streaked across the black center line into Carson territory for a feint, a fast break, and then a lay-up. Washington was proving its cockiness.

In six minutes the score was Washington–10, Carson–0.

Carson called time.

"This looks good for me," commented Coach Wilkins dryly. "You guys mad at me or something?"

None of the boys looked directly at him.

"No, sir. We just can't seem to get going," Lee Mattoon said. "They're running circles around us."

"I can see that," said the coach. "Let's have a little change here. Eric, go in for Sam. Dick, in for Eddie. Let's play basketball now. What do you say?"

The two minutes were up. The boys clapped their

hands once in unison. The five now playing trotted out onto the court. The others sat down.

Washington plunked in a long set shot. Then Eric scored. Jeff drew a foul. The quarter ended with Carson still trailing by nine points.

The second quarter was almost a replica of the first, except that Carson gathered six points. They closed the gap in the third quarter, playing close-press ball and attempting shots only from near the basket. Washington sank only two goals that quarter.

Going into the fourth period the score was Washington–42, Carson–32. Carson, a changed team since the first quarter, scored once, added two more points on foul shots, and then sank a lay-up before Washington called time. The time-out apparently helped the opponents. They sank two baskets in rapid succession. Then Carson rallied. Washington was two points ahead when the clock showed twenty seconds to go.

"Let's get that ball!" Jeff shouted.

The Washington players were passing among themselves, freezing the ball. Jeff watched his man carefully, timing the throws. Sweat glistened on his body as he waited breathlessly for the right moment.

Then he saw it—the man snapping his wrist, the ball shooting through the air. Jeff darted forward, reached out, knocked the ball down, and dribbled high and hard down the full length of the court. No Washington man was near him. He came up under the basket, raised his left leg and pushed upward with his right arm for a perfect lay-up!

The score was tied! And then the buzzer sounded.

"Beautiful play, Jeff," said Coach Wilkins, slapping him on the shoulder as the boys huddled together at the side line. "Let's take 'em in the overtime."

Jeff breathed heavily.

"Let's do it for Coach Wilkins, *and* Coach Cochran," he said.

Washington plowed through the Carson squad for the first basket breaking the tie. Then Jeff shot a long one, missing by inches. Lee took the rebound and pushed it in. Then Eddie drew a foul.

That was it. Eddie made the shot, the buzzer sounded, and the game was over.

"I'll never forget that one," said Jeff as he crowded into the bus seat later with Lee. "That was the best."

Lee grinned.

"Sure. We had to play twice as hard. We had to do it for Wilkins, and for Cochran, didn't we?"

Jeff smiled.

"That's right," he said.

It was frigid weather Saturday, and there was an inch of hard-crusted snow on the ground.

"Let's take a fly in the sky," Kevin suggested to Jeff, smiling at his own poetry.

"Okay," said Jeff.

They dressed warmly and rode out to the airport. All the way over Kevin was silent. Only once did he speak, and then only to ask how last night's game had come out.

They reached the airport. Kevin warmed up the

Champ, taxied onto the runway, and took off. They flew for half an hour. Afterwards they rode back to town and Kevin parked in front of Mike's Restaurant, where they both ordered strawberry sodas. Jeff had a feeling that there was something on Kevin's mind, something he wanted to say. Was it something about his Tuesday night activities? Jeff hadn't been able to sleep many nights for thinking about what Kevin's secret could be.

The sodas were served. Jeff took a sip. Kevin took a long pull on his, swallowed, and said, "Jeff, I've been wanting to tell you this for a long time."

Jeff met Kevin's brown eyes squarely.

"What, Kevin?"

"It was never my idea to discourage you from playing basketball, or whatever kind of sport you wanted to take up. It was Dad's idea. He urged me over and over again to try to keep your interest away from it, and I tried to do as he asked. I didn't want to upset him. You know how Dad is. I hope you understand what I'm trying to say, Jeff."

Jeff swallowed to steady himself.

"I think I do. And I'm glad you told me. I've often wondered."

Kevin laughed softly.

"I know. I've sensed it, and it's bothered me, bothered me terribly. I was glad when Dad told you to go back to playing basketball. It was a big load off my mind."

Jeff grinned. He'd never forget that evening as long as he lived.

"Was Dad hard on you, too?" Jeff asked. "Didn't he want you to play either?"

Kevin nodded.

"Exactly. And I never did."

"You never went out for any sport at all in school?"

"Nothing," said Kevin. "Dad didn't believe in it, so he didn't want me to believe in it."

"Didn't you care whether you did or not?"

"Care? Of course I cared! You know something? I wish I was ten—or twelve—or fourteen again. Like you. I'd go out for some sport. You bet your life I would. Basketball, baseball, football—even ping-pong. Why, everybody's taken up some sport or other some time in his life, Jeff. *Every*body. The fellows I work with are wonderful engineers, but they lived normal lives like other youngsters. A lot of them even stayed with athletics in college. A couple played baseball before deciding to quit and stick to engineering. I'm like an outsider up there at the lab. Can I tell them it was my father who didn't want his son to be an athlete? They would razz him to his grave!"

"That's right," said Jeff. "I guess it took Mr. Gallagher to bring Dad to his senses."

"To his senses, and to make him realize that a kid in school has to have something besides studies," said Kevin. "Sports are fun, but they're a lot more than that." He shook his head regretfully and Jeff was sympathetic. He could imagine how it must feel never to have had any experience with athletics. Maybe some guys wouldn't care. Their father certainly didn't.

But he felt sorry for guys like Kevin, who could look back and see what they'd missed.

Oh, Kevin, Jeff thought. *If only you had told Dad a long time ago that he was wrong and stuck to what you believed! But you were like me. Neither of us wanted to hurt our dad.*

And then Jeff said:

"Kevin, will you tell me something else?"

"What's that, Jeff?"

"Where do you go on Tuesday nights?"

Jeff surprised himself by asking the question. He had spoken almost without thinking. And now he wondered whether Kevin would answer honestly.

Kevin looked over the rim of the glass at him and smiled.

"Oh? You've been wondering about that?"

Jeff smiled too.

"Yeah. So has Mom. Maybe Dad has, too, unless he knows. 'Course, if you don't want to tell me—"

Kevin finished his soda, pushed the glass toward the middle of the table. "I'll tell you. Come along, my friend. I'll show you where I've been going every Tuesday night!"

Kevin paid for the sodas. He and Jeff got back into the car and rode toward the middle of Carson. Kevin parked, dropped a dime into a meter, and started across the street. Jeff followed, throbbing with anxiety.

As they reached the brick building on the opposite corner, Kevin caught Jeff's arm. He pointed at the inscription over the high archway, and Jeff blinked.

"Well, I'll be," he thought.

CHAPTER 13

"Young Men's Christian Association."

Jeff read the large words inscribed in marble and all the suspicions he had built up about Kevin melted instantly. He looked at his brother, and shame replaced bitterness.

"Boy, what a relief this is," he said, with an audible sigh. "I had all kinds of crazy thoughts about you!"

Kevin grinned.

"I was afraid you might."

"You were, and still you wouldn't tell me?"

"I wanted to keep it a secret as long as I could. I've been meaning to tell you. And Mom and Dad, too. Come on. Let's go in."

They walked up the steps and in through the tall double doors. Kevin took out his wallet and showed his membership card to a man sitting in an office.

"This is my brother," Kevin said. "He's with me."

The man smiled.

"Okay."

Kevin showed some of the rooms to Jeff. There was a library, a room with ping-pong tables, another with gymnastic equipment—bell bars, arms and leg torsion springs—a swimming pool, and finally a basketball court.

"What a place!" Jeff said excitedly. "I've always heard about the Y, but I never thought it was like this!"

"We can't go out on the floor without sneakers," said Kevin. "But this is where I've been coming every Tuesday night. Playing basketball with a bunch of guys, and then finishing it off with a swim. It's been a lot of fun."

"I'll bet!" said Jeff. "But Kevin, why didn't you tell Joan? Didn't she ever worry that you might be seeing another girl?"

Kevin laughed.

"She's known all along! I told her when I started."

"You dog!" said Jeff. "And all the time I thought—" he paused. "Oh, well, I'm not supposed to know *every-thing* that's going on!"

On the way home Jeff felt better than he had in a long time.

Sunday night Jeff studied science for an hour before going to bed. On Monday Mr. Gregory gave the class another test. Jeff caught Mr. Gregory looking at him once in a while with that familiar sour expression.

The test was one of the most difficult they'd had. After the forty-minute period was over and all the papers were in, Jeff met Gil Baker in the hall.

"What did you think of it, Gil?" Jeff asked.

Gil shook his head.

"It was tough. But do you remember any exam he's given that wasn't?"

Jeff grimaced.

"You're right. By the way, don't you wish you were back on the squad?"

Gil shrugged.

"Not really. I miss it some, but not much."

"You're a funny guy, Gil," said Jeff.

Gil laughed.

"I thought you were funny, too."

Jeff looked surprised.

"Me?"

"Yes, you. Taking flying lessons in the wintertime!"

Jeff roared.

"Oh, that! Well, I'm not taking lessons now. I will be again, though, when summer rolls around. See you."

They went in opposite directions.

In the afternoon Jeff was talking with Lee, Bruce, and Gil in the gym when suddenly there were footsteps beside them. All four boys looked around, almost in unison.

"Oh, hi, Mr. Gregory," said Lee.

Mr. Gregory's pit-like eyes traveled slowly over each boy and then settled on Jeff.

"Hi, boys," he said. And then he stabbed Jeff on the shoulder with the tip of his finger. "You," he said. "Come with me."

CHAPTER 14

Mr. Gregory led Jeff to the science room. He went to his desk, opened a drawer, then paused and looked at Jeff. Jeff was sure that if there ever was a contest for the most sour-looking teacher in the state, Mr. Gregory would take first prize.

"I thought perhaps you might be anxious to know how you did in the test we had this morning," he said.

Jeff's pulse throbbed. He had been anxious, of course, but he would never have asked Mr. Gregory outright.

"I didn't think you had the papers corrected yet," Jeff said.

"Well, I haven't. Not all of them. But I have yours."

Mr. Gregory's lids closed over his eyes, a true sign that the news he was about to impart was bad.

"Maybe you'd better not tell me," said Jeff, turning as if to go.

"On the contrary," said Mr. Gregory. "I think I'd better. Come back."

He pawed at some papers in the drawer, and brought out three sheets which Jeff recognized immediately as his science test papers. He strained to see what mark Mr. Gregory had written on the top of the first page. Sixty? Sixty-five?

"There you are," said Mr. Gregory.

Jeff's eyes widened and he caught his breath.

"Ninety-two!" he gasped.

He looked at Mr. Gregory. Unbelievably a smile slowly curled the corners of the teacher's lips, and his eyes lost their sour expression and sparkled with pleasure.

"That's right, Jeff," he said. "Ninety-two. Congratulations. Well done. You have the second highest mark, so far."

"Who has the highest?" asked Jeff.

"Gil Baker."

"Gil? Boy! Am I glad!"

Mr. Gregory nodded.

"He's been able to give more time to study since he dropped basketball. He had to if he wanted to continue with six subjects. He's become a much better student. Fortunately Gil didn't mind too much dropping the game. At least, that's what he says. What do you think, Jeff? Think Gil misses it?"

Jeff shrugged.

"I don't know. He's told us, too, that he doesn't. But I know it was hard for Gil to play basketball and keep up with his studies. And he wants to try for scholarships to help him through college because his folks can't afford to send him."

"Gil's working hard. He'll make it. As for you—" He paused. "Who're you playing tomorrow night?"

"Brighton."

Mr. Gregory put out his slender white hand. Jeff took it, felt Mr. Gregory's firm grip.

"Destroy them," Mr. Gregory said. "Not savagely, of course. But by the rules."

Jeff was astounded. But he felt overjoyed as he left the room. That Mr. Gregory! He's a real human being after all! And I thought he was a stupe! Maybe Mr. Gallagher talked to him, too.

"What did he want with you?" Bruce asked when Jeff walked back into the gym. "Did he tell you he's failed you so that you can't play tomorrow night?"

Jeff narrowed his eyes.

"Nope. Matter of fact, just the opposite. He told me I got ninety-two in the test this morning, and said we should destroy Brighton."

Lee Mattoon did a playful double take; then he shook his head.

"I don't think I'll ever know that guy if I live to be a hundred."

"And you," Jeff said to Gil, "you beat me."

"Me?" Gil stared, open-mouthed. "I got over ninety-two?"

"Yes, you got over ninety-two. I don't know what, but it's the highest mark in the class so far."

"I'm glad to hear it," said Lee. "You can even beat me in English, I don't care."

Gil laughed.

Soon the buzzer sounded, ending the noon hour. The boys got up and went off to their classrooms.

At five-thirty the following evening, Jeff was beginning to worry. His father hadn't come home yet from the laboratory and in fifteen minutes he would have to leave so as to be in uniform by six o'clock. He didn't want to go without knowing definitely whether his dad was going to the game or not. Kevin had ridden home with someone else, so he didn't know what time his father would be home.

A few minutes later a car drove up to the curb in front of the house. Jeff, watching eagerly out the window, saw that it was his father.

Mr. Dooley came into the house through the living room door.

"Hi, Jeff . . . Kevin . . . Mother."

"Hello, Dad."

"Going to the game, Dad?" Jeff asked expectantly.

Mr. Dooley removed his coat and hat and hung them in the closet.

"Look, son, there are other games, aren't there? You'll be playing again next week, won't you? Maybe I can see that one. At any rate, I can't tonight. Sam Pierson is coming over and we're going back to the lab at seven o'clock. Another project has come up—a very important one—and our deadline is next Tuesday. That doesn't give us much time."

Jeff's heart sank.

"Okay, Dad," he said. "Tonight's our last game. But we'll be in the playoffs. Anyway, I guess that new project is more important than going to a basketball game."

"I should hope so," said Mr. Dooley. He turned around, rubbing his palms. "How's supper coming, Mother?"

Mrs. Dooley was standing in the doorway.

"It's ready now," she said woodenly. She gave her husband a long hard look, then turned and went back into the kitchen.

Jeff ate very little. Later, Kevin drove him to school.

"Don't feel bad about Dad," said Kevin. "He'll just never understand what it means to you, Jeff. Or to me, either."

"But I wanted him to come tonight very much," said Jeff. "I wanted him to see what the game was like. I wanted him to know why I feel the way I do about it."

Kevin nodded. "Maybe Mom and I can work on Dad. Especially Mom. She's got more influence with Dad than anybody else."

"I doubt that you'll have any luck," said Jeff. "That new project Dad is working on now is the most important thing in the world to him. He's not going to skip a night of working on that just to see *me* play basketball."

"We'll see," said Kevin. "Good luck, brother."

"You're coming, aren't you?" Jeff shouted as Kevin started to drive away.

"You bet!" Kevin yelled back. The next second the exhaust spurted a cloud of smoke as the car whisked away from the curb.

Jeff hurried through the door of the school, down the long corridor already clogged with early arrivers, and down the stairs to the locker room.

"Well!" said Bruce Parker. "About time you got here, kid. I thought you'd quit again."

Jeff grinned.

"I got here as soon as I could," he said.

He undressed, got into his uniform, and climbed the stairs to the gym. He felt tense and nervous.

Someone threw him a ball. He caught it, dribbled in, shot. The ball bounced off the backboard, struck the rim, rolled off.

He glanced often at the bleachers. Kids were filing in on one side, mostly kids from junior high. Parents were flocking in, too. He saw Bruce's mother and father, and Eric's, and Lee Mattoon's.

But even Kevin hadn't shown up yet.

At twenty-five past six, Coach Cochran called the boys together. The coach was feeling better. His bandages had been removed.

"Brighton's an improved team since the last time we played them," Cochran said. "They've got a new center, a boy about six-feet-two, who's been making quite a name for himself as a rebounder. His name's Fredericks. Lee, he's your man, but we all have to get in there and play the best brand of basketball we know. I'm not going to preach to you how to play basketball. You know the game. Just get in there, pass fast, make baskets. If Brighton starts rallying, call time as soon as you can. Okay. Good luck."

The buzzer sounded. The teams got together on the court, shook hands, checked each other's numbers. Jeff's man was Number 16, a tall dark-haired boy with freckles under his eyes.

Jeff glanced hopefully at the bleachers again. But the faces were a blur. There were so many people now he couldn't tell whether his family had come or not.

But then he saw a woman in a dark blue coat walk in through the door. Behind her was a man in a tan winter coat, and another, a taller younger man—in a gray tweed topcoat. They were peering anxiously out onto the court. And then they looked directly at Jeff.

Jeff responded with an excited wave. They had all come—Mom, Dad, and Kevin!

The referee blew his whistle. The ball sailed straight up into the air between the two centers. The two tall men leaped, their right arms stretched high above their heads. Fredericks tapped the ball. A Brighton player caught it, dribbled back, then worked the ball cautiously to the front of the court.

Bruce got in front of him and tried to take the ball away. The player stopped, pivoted, and shot an overhand pass. It was meant for Fredericks, but Lee stuck out his hand, knocked the ball down, and passed to Jeff. Jeff dribbled down court and heaved a pass to Bruce. Bruce passed to Sam Bullick. Sam went up for a lay-up and missed. Jeff leaped, tried to tap in the rebound. He missed, too. He leaped again, but a pair of long arms reached up and took the ball. It was Fredericks.

The tall center spun and threw an overhand pass up court. Another Brighton player caught the ball, dribbled in fast, and went high for the lay-up.

Two points!

The Brighton jayvees' cheerleaders, dressed in sparkling red and white uniforms, stamped their feet and cheered wildly.

Carson took out the ball. Eddie passed to Sam. Sam

dribbled across the center line, passed to Jeff. Jeff worked the ball in closer to the basket, watching out for Number 16 who was guarding him closely. Suddenly he saw an opening and charged in. Two Brighton men swooped on him. Jeff raised his left knee, pushing himself off the floor with his right leg. He brought the ball up with both hands.

Smack!

The whistle shrilled. Foul!

"Nice going, Jeff," said Lee. "Make it."

Jeff walked to the free-throw line, panting for breath, his father was probably wondering why Jeff had been given a chance to make a basket. He didn't know anything about fouls, free throws, double dribble, traveling, or pushing. He didn't know a thing about basketball.

A new worry disturbed Jeff's thoughts. He wondered why it hadn't occurred to him before. What good was it to have his father watch this game? He would sit on that hard seat through it all, bored stiff. He wouldn't care to see another game if Carson had the best team in the league—because he wouldn't know what was going on.

CHAPTER 15

JEFF ACCEPTED the ball from the referee. He placed his toes close to the free-throw line, spread his legs slightly apart, and measured the basket with his eyes. For that one moment the gym was silent.

Jeff dipped his knees, brought the ball down slowly, and then up. He snapped his wrists. The ball arched toward the basket. Swish! It riffled through the net.

Brighton took out the ball and worked it swiftly to their forecourt. Number 16 flitted around like a dragonfly. Jeff had difficulty keeping track of him. He was too late to block a pass to 16, and saw his man dribble in and make the lay-up. The ball went over to Carson. In his hurry, Lee heaved a pass point-blank at a Brighton player who squirted in like a pumpkin seed. Bruce bolted in on the play and the referee tweeked his whistle for a jump ball.

Brighton caught the tap. In swift short passes the ball zigzagged across the center line toward the Brighton basket. Jeff whirled after his man. Near the basket he anticipated the play. Fredericks had taken the ball down the corner. He faked a set shot, then whipped an overhand pass to 16. Just as he went into motion Jeff rushed in front of his man, knocked the ball down, caught the bounce, spun, and passed the ball to Sam Bullick.

Sam rifled a pass to Bruce, and Bruce to Lee. Lee made a fast break for a lay-up, soared up high, and pushed the ball against the backboard. The ball sank through the hoop as bodies collided.

"Number 6!" shouted the referee, pointing at a Brighton man. "One shot! Basket counts!"

The Carson cheerleaders screamed. The fans burst into a round of applause.

"No!" yelled the Brighton coach.

The referee ignored him. Lee walked nonchalantly to the free-throw line. The official tossed him the ball. Calmly, nimbly, Lee sank the shot. Brighton took out the ball. In three swift passes it was down the other end of the court. Then swish! Brighton scored.

Carson took the ball from out of bounds, moved it down their end of the court, and Sam scored with a set shot from the corner. Brighton evened it up by sinking a similar shot.

As the first quarter went into its final seconds, Jeff realized that Coach Cochran was right. Brighton was a better team than it had been in the first game with Carson. They were matching Carson almost score for score. But when the buzzer sounded Carson was ahead by one point, 14–13.

Eric started in place of Eddie in the second period. He went into the game with his hair combed neatly back, but after a minute of play some of it had fallen loose over his ear. He was in there, playing hard. Jeff grinned to himself. The coach must've said something to him.

Fre-e-e-e-e-t! Foul on Number 7. Eric!

Eric glared at the referee.

"Easy, Eric," cautioned Jeff.

Brighton made the basket. Carson took the ball out and moved it down court. Like lightning a Brighton player swooped in and intercepted it. Brighton brought it back up court. Number 16 caught a throw in front of Jeff, faked a pass, and then leaped for a hook shot. The ball missed. Jeff turned and jumped high for the rebound. Another pair of hands grasped the ball, too. But coming down Jeff yanked hard for its possession, got the ball, and dribbled out of the tight spot. He heaved a pass to Eric, and Eric passed to Bruce. Jeff raced along the side line. Bruce shot him the ball. Jeff caught it, faked for the basket as his man came bolting up, and then broke fast for the net. Up he shot. The ball bounced off the backboard and into the net for two points.

Then Carson began to hit hard. Jeff and Lee sank three apiece before the startled Brighton team called time.

Dick Mizner went in for Bruce, and Bill Godell replaced Eric. Jeff saw that the margin had spread in favor of Carson. He purposely stood with his back to the bench so that he could look across the court at his family. He saw them. His mother's face was bright with a smile. Evidently she was enjoying the game. He wasn't sure how his father felt. Kevin was talking to him, and once in a while his father nodded his head.

He hoped Kevin was explaining the game as they went along.

Then Jeff saw his father turn to the person at his other side. It was Mr. Gallagher, the principal! He, too, seemed to be having an enjoyable time.

Time-in was called. Brighton had the ball. They took it out and moved it quickly to their forecourt, pressing toward the basket. The ball got loose. Jeff and Fredericks bolted after it. They reached it together, locking their arms around it. Fredericks shook it frantically, trying to jerk the ball from Jeff. Jeff hung on tightly.

"Jump ball," the referee called.

Jeff and Fredericks faced each other. Jeff waited tensely. If he could tap the ball as it went up—

But he didn't. He didn't have a chance. After the referee tossed the ball up, Fredericks tapped it. Brighton took the ball and worked it close to their basket. Jeff rushed in fast as a Brighton man tried for another two points. He missed. Jeff went up high, caught the rebound, and flipped the ball to Lee. Carson moved the ball hurriedly to their forecourt, Dick Mizner and Lee in on the play. Lee passed to Dick under the net and Dick went up for a lay-up.

When the half ended, Carson led, 31–22.

The boys felt good as they toweled the sweat off and rested in the locker room. Brighton had faltered in that second period. They weren't really better than they had been before.

"Don't get too cocky, though," Coach Cochran warned his boys. "I'd hate to see those guys come back and snap the game out from under you. That has been known to happen, you know."

Jeff wasn't especially worried about the outcome of the game. He was thinking about his father. How was he reacting to the game? Did he like the action? Did he like seeing a basket made? Was there anything at all about the game that he liked? I sure hope so, thought Jeff. How can I keep playing basketball if Dad hates me to do it? How can I ever make him understand that what Mr. Gallagher said was true: there's something about basketball that's good for kids. It isn't just a body builder; it helps train your mind, too. Jeff remembered what Coach Cochran had told the team at the start of the season. He had said that basketball develops your thinking processes, your alertness and your coordination. If you never played basketball again after you left high school, something from the game would have rubbed off, something that would be of use later on in life. Those are the things Dad really doesn't know about, Jeff said to himself. Maybe, if he did, he would feel different.

The same five men who had begun the game started the second half. Carson sank a basket within thirty seconds. Then they scored another. They were grinning cockily now, feeling secure of their lead.

And then Brighton came awake. They took chances, attempting shots ten to fifteen feet from their basket. And they were making good. The red lights on the visitor's side of the scoreboard kept flashing, climbing higher and higher, while those on the home side remained unchanged, as if the switch were stuck.

"Let's go!" Jeff shouted. "Come on, men! Let's go!"

But attempts to rally the team didn't help. By the end of the third quarter the score was tied, and the gym was a bedlam. Cheerleaders from both sides seemed to be trying to outdo each other in volume.

"I hate to say I told you so," said Coach Cochran grimly. "But you saw what happened. Now get in there this last quarter and play as you did that first half. You're better than they are. Think it—and you'll prove it."

The buzzer sounded. Carson had the ball. They moved it cautiously down the court. Bruce caught a pass near the corner, looked for someone to pass to, saw no one, then shot. The ball hit the rim, bounded off.

Hands shot up to grab the rebound. One, reaching higher, poked the ball. Back up it went and rolled over the edge of the rim. Swish! A basket!

Now Brighton had the ball. They moved it across the court. A pass, a fake, and then a charge toward the hoop.

Two points!

The Brighton team was holding its own. A minute went by. Two minutes. Three.

Score: Carson–52, Brighton–51.

Four minutes went by: Carson–56, Brighton–59.

Four minutes and a half: Carson–58, Brighton–61.

Brighton called time. Jeff was glad. Except for two or three minutes, he had played the entire game. He was sweating and breathing hard.

"Boy!" he gasped. "I'm bushed!"

"Me, too," said Lee. "How much more time do we have?"

"Three and a half minutes," someone said.

All five men sat on the floor. Coach Cochran tapped Jeff on the knee.

"You and Lee stay out for a minute. Get some rest. Eric and Jim will go in."

"I'm all right," said Jeff. "I can—"

"You heard me," said the coach.

Actually, Jeff was thankful for the extra minute of rest. Brighton tallied another point by virtue of a foul on Eric, and then Jim Barclay scored one to bring Carson back up to within two points of Brighton.

With a little more than two minutes left in the game, Jeff and Lee went back in. Brighton took out the ball, but lost it when one of their men was called on traveling.

Bruce took the ball from out of bounds, passed to Eddie. Eddie passed to Jeff. Jeff dribbled cautiously down mid-court toward his forecourt. Number 16, barging in, tried to slap the ball away. Jeff lifted the ball, passed to Lee near the basket, and charged across the free-throw line. Lee faked a throw for the basket, drawing the guards away from Jeff, then flipped an over-the-head pass to Jeff. Jeff caught it, leaped high. He lifted the ball straight up in front of him. It cleared the edge of the rim and riffled through the net.

The Carson fans screamed. The score was 62–62.

With only a minute and a half left to play, Brighton took the ball from out of bounds and hurried it quickly across the center line. Carson, playing a man-to-man defense, forced the Brighton players to weave in all directions as they tried to get the ball closer to their basket. Then a Brighton man tried a set shot and made it.

With the game in favor of Brighton now, Carson worked the ball swiftly to their forecourt. Bruce dribbled across the center line, and bounce-passed to Jeff. Jeff, taking the ball behind the free-throw line, pivoted and arched a pass toward the basket. It struck the backboard. The Carson fans roared as the ball just missed the hoop.

Then up went a long white arm. Long slender fingers tapped the ball. It went in!

"Thataway, Lee!" shouted Jeff.

Thirty-five seconds to go, and the score was tied again.

Brighton took the ball out and moved down court. Bruce plunged in. Smack!

Tre-e-e-e-k! It was a foul called on Bruce.

Jeff shook his head. He watched the Brighton man take his place at the free-throw line, accept the ball from the referee, and aim carefully for the basket.

He shot, arching the ball beautifully. It dropped with a soft whisper through the hoop.

Carson brought the ball out, rushed it swiftly to their forecourt. Time was running out fast.

And then suddenly the game was over. The buzzer sounded loud and clear, announcing the end.

Brighton had won, 65–64.

For a while there were joyous screams from the Brighton fans. Cheerleaders from both teams got on the floor together and joined hands in a yell. Players grasped each other's hands. On one side were the happy smiles of victory, on the other the sad faces of defeat.

"It was a good game," Bruce said in the locker room. "But we should've won."

Jeff showered, then dressed quietly. They had lost, but to a good team. Brighton had done well. The game could have gone either way. That was the way to look at it. And there were still the playoffs. Perhaps Carson would meet Brighton again.

But Jeff was mainly concerned about his father. I wonder what he's thinking, thought Jeff. Maybe he doesn't care. Maybe watching the game was just a waste of time for him.

Jeff rose to go. "Well—see you guys," he said.

"Wait a minute, Jeff."

Coach Cochran was coming into the locker room. Behind him was the coach of the varsity team, Harris Wilkins.

"I've got some news for you, Jeff," said Stu Cochran. "I'll let Coach Wilkins tell you."

Jeff looked curiously from Cochran to Wilkins. His heart pounded.

"News?" he echoed.

"That's right," said the varsity coach, smiling. "Every year, you know, we select a player or two from the jayvees to move up to the varsity. He starts in the varsity playoffs, and from there on he's on the varsity team. This year Stu and I got our heads together and decided that of all the players you're the most eligible. Not only have you shown remarkable ability as a basketball player, Jeff, but you've also proven yourself a good sport. I've heard a lot of fans say the same things about you, so it's something others have recognized in you, too."

He put out his hand. Jeff took it.

"Congratulations, Jeff."

Jeff's throat tightened. "Thanks, coach," he said.

And then he saw a pair of familiar faces—his father's, Kevin's, and behind them, Mr. Gallagher's.

His father came forward, extending a hand proudly. A flicker of a smile was on his lips.

"I don't think I have to say anything, son," he said. "Matter of fact, I—I can't very well now, anyway. Mr. Wilkins said it all. He said it better than anybody could. At least, I heard every word, and I'm in complete agreement. Are you ready to go? Your mother's waiting for us."

A smile touched Jeff's lips.

"I'm ready, Dad. Hi, Mr. Gallagher," he said as he walked in front of the principal.

"Hi, Jeff," said Mr. Gallagher. "Nice game, and congratulations."

"Thanks," Jeff said.

He walked up the stairs ahead of his father and Kevin. His mother was waiting in the hall. They walked out together, his mother's arm linked through his. From the corner of his eye he could see her smiling proudly at him. Mr. Dooley began to talk excitedly about the game, the first he'd ever seen in his life.

He's on my side now, thought Jeff. I'll have nothing to worry about any more, except making baskets.